W9-BYR-992

Tell Me Who

JESSICA WOLLMAN

Dutton Children's Books

♡ *Dutton Children's Books* ♡
A DIVISION OF PENGUIN YOUNG READERS GROUP

Published by the Penguin Group
Penguin Group (USA) Inc., 375 Hudson Street, New York, New York 10014, U.S.A. ♡ Penguin Group (Canada), 90 Eglinton Avenue East, Suite 700, Toronto, Ontario M4P 2Y3, Canada (a division of Pearson Penguin Canada Inc.) ♡ Penguin Books Ltd, 80 Strand, London WC2R 0RL, England Penguin Ireland, 25 St Stephen's Green, Dublin 2, Ireland (a division of Penguin Books Ltd) ♡ Penguin Group (Australia), 250 Camberwell Road, Camberwell, Victoria 3124, Australia (a division of Pearson Australia Group Pty Ltd) ♡ Penguin Books India Pvt Ltd, 11 Community Centre, Panchsheel Park, New Delhi - 110 017, India ♡ Penguin Group (NZ), 67 Apollo Drive, Rosedale, North Shore 0632, New Zealand (a division of Pearson New Zealand Ltd.) ♡ Penguin Books (South Africa) (Pty) Ltd, 24 Sturdee Avenue, Rosebank, Johannesburg 2196, South Africa ♡ Penguin Books Ltd, Registered Offices: 80 Strand, London WC2R 0RL, England

Library of Congress Cataloging-in-Publication Data
Wollman, Jessica.
Tell me who / Jessica Wollman.—1st ed. p. cm.
Summary: Two sixth-grade girls obsessed with fortune telling discover a machine that tells them who they—and anyone else—are destined to marry.
ISBN 978-0-525-42087-3
[1. Fortune telling—Fiction. 2. Best friends—Fiction. 3.Friendship—Fiction.] I. Title.
PZ7.W8355Te 2009 [Fic]—dc22 2008013895

Published in the United States by Dutton Children's Books,
A division of Penguin Young Readers Group
345 Hudson Street, New York, New York 10014
www.penguin.com/youngreaders

DESIGNED BY ABBY KUPERSTOCK

Printed in USA ♡ First Edition
1 3 5 7 9 10 8 6 4 2

For Dan,
the best "who"

ACKNOWLEDGMENTS

Many many thanks to . . .
Sarah Shumway, Stephanie Lurie,
Deborah Kaplan, Abby Kuperstock,
and the entire team at Dutton for
all of their hard work and terrific insights.
Richard Abate for his support (and sale!);
Matt and Jen Kraft for the great title;
Caroline Wallace for the fab photo.
And, of course, my family and friends
for putting up with all of my
"can't talk, gotta write" nonsense.

Tell Me Who

Chapter 1

"QUIT MOVING IT."

"I'm *not*!"

The indicator on my brand-new Ouija board is freaking out, slipping and sliding all over the place. In less than five minutes, I've heard from both sets of great grandparents and a spirit named "Irene," who promises that my hair will naturally straighten on my sixteenth birthday.

I roll back on my heels and glance across the board, where my best friend, Tanna Walker, sits cross-legged on the floor of my bedroom.

"I can feel your fingers *pushing*," I tell her.

"Molly, has it ever occurred to you that the board might actually work?"

I shake my head.

"Why not?"

"Because we bought it at Toys "Я" Us. And it's made by some weirdo named Psychic Steve." I point to the bottom left corner of the board, where the Psychic Steve logo is printed. It's a picture of Steve himself—or at least his super-round, super-red face. His hair's gray and wiry and his cheeks are puffy, like a chipmunk's, except not at all cute looking. It's too bad Psychic Steve didn't ask around before he slapped his face on all those Ouija boards. Calling on spirits is spooky enough without his big old moon head staring up at you.

Tanna flips her straight blond hair off of her face. She does this a lot, because she says her hair is her best feature and it's important to draw attention to your best feature. According to Tanna, my skin is my best feature, but I'm not really sure why. Or how I can draw any more attention to it other than by walking around naked, which is so not happening.

Tanna sighs. "Okay, fine. Maybe I did give it a little tap. You know, just to warm it up."

We look at each other for a couple more seconds and then burst out laughing.

"Who's Irene?" I ask, when we finally come up for air.

She shrugs. "I just wanted to give you some good news about the Frizz."

Tanna calls my hair the Frizz because she swears it has no idea it's actually attached to the rest of my body. No matter how many times I brush it, the curls just frizz up and do whatever they want. And I have to wear it army short, because if I wait too long between haircuts, I end up looking like I've got a bright red LEGO sitting on top of my head. I don't really mind *so* much, but Tanna thinks the Frizz is such a big problem I should have my own reality TV show: *Curls Gone Wild*.

The Frizz is definitely *not* my best feature.

Tanna clasps her hands behind her back and leans forward, stretching. "So now what? Wanna try Light as a Feather, Stiff as a Board again?"

"It's really not a two-person game," I point out.

"It's not a *game*, Molly, it's a psychic exercise," Tanna says. She reaches up to dim the lights, then scoots toward

me. "And the number of people doesn't matter. You just have to do it right."

I groan but stretch out on the floor and lay my head in her lap. I learned a long time ago that it's stupid to argue with Tanna when she fixes her mind on something. She's just way too good at getting what she wants.

Tanna and I have been best friends since the first grade, when I walked into the bathroom and Chloe Janes took one look at me and shrieked, "You're not allowed in here. This is the *girls'* room." I just stood there, wishing my hair would sprout down to my knees and trying really hard not to cry. And then Tanna stepped out of the stall and grabbed my hand. Just like that. "She is *too* a girl," she told Chloe. "And you're just dumb."

"Okay, now relax," Tanna instructs, placing her hands on either side of my face. Her fingers draw soft circles around my temples as she whispers, "Light as a feather, stiff as a board. Light as a feather, stiff as a board."

I close my eyes and let my arms and legs sink in to the carpet, which is actually a lot itchier than it looks. The stiff little hairs keep poking me in the back and I wiggle around, trying to get more comfortable.

“Quit moving,” she orders. “You have to focus or this won’t work.”

“Quit telling me what to do,” I shoot back.

Tanna sighs but goes back to chanting, “Light as a feather, stiff as a board.” I keep my eyes closed and listen to the sound of her voice and the wind whipping against the window. A cozy little shiver runs down my spine as I think about how nice it is to be inside. Even if I am lying on the floor.

“Light as a feather, stiff as a board,” Tanna repeats. Her voice sounds sort of fuzzy now, and really far away. My back drops deeper into the rug, which suddenly feels a lot softer. Almost slippery. Everything feels soft and slippery.

And then it doesn’t.

“Ow!” I yelp as Tanna’s hands grip under my arm, jerking me up. The top half of my body lifts slightly, then flops back against the carpet with a loud thud. I press my hand to my head, which really, really hurts.

Tanna’s standing over me, looking worried but also a little excited. “Are you okay? Do you need ice?”

“What were you *doing*?” I ask, sitting up. My mouth feels all prickly.

"I think it really worked this time," Tanna gushes. Her cheeks are flushed and her eyes jackrabbit around the room. "I mean, you definitely went . . . *somewhere*. I could sense it. So I tried to lift you and that's when the trance or whatever must have broken . . ."

"It wasn't a trance," I tell her. "I was *sleeping*."

"Are you sure?" Tanna insists. "Maybe you just don't know what psychic vibrations feel like."

"I know what sleeping feels like," I point out. "I do that every night."

Tanna toys with a brown crystal dangling from her neck. She wears three on the same chain, since crystals represent a positive future. "But my tigereye was totally flashing—which makes sense since it's, like, a spiritual protector."

I raise my eyebrows. "A *what*?"

"I swear there was *a presence*," she insists, shooting me a hopeful look. "Did you feel *anything*?"

I shake my head. "Nope. Just tired." Tanna's eyes snap back to normal and I can tell she's disappointed. I wish we could just forget the whole thing, but I do feel sort of bad about falling asleep when I was supposed to be making all kinds of psychic connections. So after a few seconds I add, "We could check the tarot cards, I guess."

"Good idea," Tanna says, perking up as she reaches into her bag. "If there were any spirits hanging around they'll be, like, supercharged. We'll get a really good reading."

"What's that for?" I ask, pointing at the deck. It's wrapped in a red silk scarf I've never seen before.

"It protects their aura," Tanna explains as she starts to shuffle. She places the pack on the carpet and taps them with her crystals. "This should help, too."

I rest my chin in my hand and try really hard to look interested, even though I have no idea what aura she's talking about and sort of wish we were baking brownies or watching TV instead.

Ever since her Aunt Liza gave her the cards for her birthday, Tanna's been on a huge fortune-telling kick. It's all she wants to do anymore. She even visited a psychic, the Amazing Maureen, but it didn't really work out. Maureen's booth is in the food court at Montgomery Mall, right next to the Hamburger Connection, and Tanna's a strict vegetarian. She said the smell of frying cows made her sick.

"Okay," Tanna says importantly, cutting the deck into three separate piles. "Does Molly have a secret admirer?"

I shoot her a look. "Hey, I thought we were gonna ask about Light as a Feather, Stiff as a Board?"

"We have to do a warm-up reading first." Tanna draws seven cards from the middle pile and places them faceup on the rug. She stares down at the pictures, chewing her lip in a worried sort of way.

"What?" I ask. I've sat through a ton of readings over the past few months but still feel a little nervous. It would probably help if I learned how to read the cards myself, but I can't. I've tried. All the symbols run together and I get them all mixed up. Besides, the pictures make absolutely no sense. I mean, what does a guy balancing seven swords have to do with being responsible? It's not like he's polishing the swords or color-coding them or anything.

"We-ell," Tanna says slowly, pointing at an image of a hand holding some sort of crystal ball with a star in the middle. "That's the seven of pentacles. It means you're gonna get rich. Really rich."

"Oh," I say, feeling relieved. "That's good."

"And there's your secret admirer." She points at a card with a naked man and woman standing in front of a swirly background. "The lovers card. That's *great*."

My stomach tightens. I shift my eyes away from the naked people and try not to think about the word *lover*. Or my secret admirer.

"But here's what's sort of weird," Tanna continues, waving her hand over three cards. "That's the ace of wands, the empress, and the princess of disks."

"So what?"

"Well, alone, they're sort of cool," she says, running her fingers through her hair. "The ace of wands means, like, a new beginning. The empress represents abundance, and the princess of disks tells me you're trustworthy and reliable. But the thing is, together . . ." She trails off, shaking her head sadly.

I swallow. "What? What do they mean?"

Tanna bites her lip and her eyes start to dance. "Pregnancy."

I glare at her. "*What?* You're kidding, right?"

"No, I swear!" Tanna's mouth is all pinched up and I can tell she's trying really hard not to laugh.

"It's not *funny*," I say, folding my arms across my chest.

"Oh relax, Molly. It's not like it's gonna happen *now*, but—"

"Hello!" I shout, cutting her off. "I'm only twelve. It's *impossible*."

"Don't get mad at me. It's not *my* fault," Tanna says, still smirking. "I don't control the cards. I'm just the messenger."

I slump back against the bed, feeling frustrated and annoyed. It's not that I don't want to read the future. It'd be great to know when my next Algebra quiz is or if I'll finally be invited to one of Sophie Kravitz's pool parties. She had one right around Halloween and asked almost every girl in my grade except me. If I'd known about it ahead of time maybe it wouldn't have hurt so much.

So yes, I definitely can see how the whole future-telling thing would come in handy. But lately Tanna's gone a little overboard. She's definitely obsessed.

"It's not my fault," she repeats, twisting the chunky topaz ring around her index finger. It's pretty ugly—the color sort of reminds me of flat Coke—but it's Tanna's birthstone and she refuses to take it off. According to Tanna, she's a classic Scorpio: passionate and highly emotional with very deep feelings and intense interests. Out of respect for the sign, she only wears approved Scorpio colors: red, black, blue, or green.

I'm a Libra and that means I'm supposed to be very chic and elegant, which is a total joke. I never think about what I wear and I hate shopping. Seriously. The mall makes me sleepy. Plus, I'm a total klutz. I'm the only person I know who needs a tutor for PE. No matter what sport we're playing, my teacher, Mrs. Sixsmith, makes me stay behind for extra help. And I always get a C. Always.

Tanna thinks I'm not a typical Libra, because my mom died when I was seven. She says that traumatic events can stunt your spiritual development. Plus, most girls learn style and grace from their mothers, but I got cheated since mine died when I was too little for that stuff.

I guess I did get cheated. But I don't really care about the style or grace thing. Or even about being a Libra.

"Forget it," I tell her. "Let's just do something else."

Tanna rolls her eyes in a *whatever* sort of way and gathers up the cards. "Fine. Like what?"

I'm about to suggest we play Businesswoman, which is a pretend game we haven't played in months and is actually

sort of fun, when the Claw pushes my bedroom door open. I know it's the Claw even before I see her. My dad always knocks.

The Claw is my dad's girlfriend. Oops, I mean *fiancée*. Her real name is Phyllis, but Tanna and I call her the Claw because of her fingernails. They're long and Wolverine sharp; we're pretty sure they can slice cans. The Claw paints them pink, red, or white. She says she chooses the color depending on her mood, but I don't believe her. The Claw really only has one mood: *nightmare*.

I think you can learn a lot about a person by just looking at their nails. Mine are short and color-free, plain but very kidlike. Tanna likes to paint each of her nails a different Scorpio color, which is cool and original. The Claw, on the other hand, has sharp, mean-looking nails, like weapons. They fit her perfectly.

"Hi, girls," she says. "Everything okay up here? Just thought I'd check in." Whenever the Claw talks to Tanna and me, her voice gets really high, like someone's poking her in the back. She also speaks way too slowly and overenunciates all of her words. I mentioned this to my dad once and he said that the Claw isn't used to spending time with kids, and that I need to be patient with her.

That was over a year ago.

Tanna and I exchange a look. The Claw's always hassling us about our after-school activities. She thinks we spend way too much time up in my room when we could be playing outside, exercising in the fresh air (her words, not mine).

I've tried to explain that there's a big difference between being in the sixth grade and being six years old, but the Claw just doesn't get it.

Besides, Tanna and I know the truth. She just wants us out of the house so she can have the place to herself.

"We're good," I say as the Ouija catches my eye. For some reason, I know that this is something the Claw shouldn't see. Slowly, I nudge it under the bed with my foot.

Big mistake. The movement just draws her attention to the board.

"What's that?" she asks. She tries to step closer, but her pencil-thin heels are so sharp they sink into the carpet like it's grass.

Tanna leans forward and snaps the board shut.

"School project," she says.

I send her a telepathic thank-you.

The Claw straightens and folds her arms across her chest. I can tell she's debating whether or not to demand an explanation. After a few more seconds tick by her mouth twists into a smile so fake she might as well not have bothered.

"I was just wondering about your homework," she says.

Tanna points to the closed Ouija board. "We're on it."

The Claw straightens and pats her dark brown hair. "Well, then I guess I don't need to wonder, do I?"

Tanna and I shake our heads and watch as the Claw leaves the room. We wait until she clicks down the stairs. (You know what I said about people and their nails? Well, ditto for shoes.) Then we start to giggle.

The sound of the garage door opening makes me straighten.

"Think she'll tell my dad?" I ask.

Tanna holds out the tarot cards. "There's really only one way to know for sure."

I groan and flop backward onto the floor, hitting the bruise on my head.

Chapter 2

AT DINNER, MY father places a bottle of champagne in the middle of the table. "Well, Molly," he says, smiling. "Phyllis and I have a big announcement."

"What?" I ask, studying the champagne. It looks sort of weird just sitting there, between the hamburger buns and a jar of pickles. Way too fancy. It's like wearing a prom dress to go sledding.

"We set a date," the Claw says, roping her arm around my father's and sinking her nails into the sleeve of his shirt.

They're smiling these really stupid smiles and staring at me, like I'm supposed to start cheering or something.

I pick up my turkey burger and look at them. "A what?"

"A *date*," the Claw repeats in her I-know-English-is-such-a-difficult-language-to-learn voice.

I shake my head and pretend to take a bite out of my burger but really only eat the bun and some lettuce. I can't stand the Claw's cooking. She pours these really weird sauces over everything. She says they're gourmet, but I don't care. They're disgusting.

My father and I used to order Chinese food every night. The paper takeout bag was our napkin and tablecloth. Then, about two years ago, his law firm hired the Claw to redecorate their office. She liked the job so much, she decided to redecorate my dad, too. Now he wears these matching ties and shirts that are so bright, they look like Skittles. And we haven't had Chinese food in almost a year and a half.

My father fiddles with the wire basket thing at the top of the champagne bottle. "Molly, Phyllis and I have set a date for our *wedding*." When he pulls out the cork, the pop is so loud I drop my burger and jump out of my chair. The sound rings in my ears as I lean over to scrape the food off the floor.

"We're getting married in October," he says. "In the backyard."

The backyard? How boring can you get? I thought weddings were supposed to be special, held in cool places. Like on a cruise. Or in Hawaii. Or on a cruise to Hawaii.

I picture the backyard, with my rusty old swing set and the huge, drooping crab apple tree that sheds smelly fruit all over the place. Maybe the Claw will get bonked on the head with an apple during the ceremony.

I straighten slowly and sit back down, wiping my mouth with a napkin. I'm stalling. My dad and the Claw are waiting for me to congratulate them. Or smile. Or something.

But I can't. The best I can come up with is, "October's really far away. That's like ten months, right?"

My dad raises his eyebrows. "It's sooner than you think, Mol."

The Claw places her fingertips lightly on the sides of her forehead. Her bright red nails look like kebab skewers. "Don't remind me. I've got *so* much to do." She clears her throat and turns, looking straight at me. "You know, I'll be gone a lot more now."

I smile. Now *that's* something to get excited about.

But the Claw's still staring at me.

"I'm not going to be around to babysit," she says.

"I don't need a babysitter," I point out. "I've been staying by myself since I was ten."

"Mitch, *please*."

This is outrageously annoying for two reasons: One, the Claw is ignoring me completely, like I haven't said a word. And two: She's calling my father Mitch. His real name is Mitchell. As in M-I-T-C-H-E-L-L. Nobody calls him Mitch. He used to hate it when people called him Mitch. He'd make this really sour face and say, "Did you hear that, Molly? The guy *Mitched* me!" and then we'd laugh about it for an hour.

Okay, maybe not for an hour. But we'd laugh. And now my father's getting Mitched by his own fiancée—she Mitches him *all the time*—and he doesn't even *blink*. Instead of looking at *her* with his sour face, he's looking at me—his own flesh and blood—with this weird frown.

"Phyllis has a point, Molly," he says. "Her plate is kind of full."

The Claw pouts. "Planning a wedding is a full-time job. Plus, I've got my business to run."

Last fall, the Claw quit her job with the interior design firm to become an antiques dealer. But as far as I can tell,

she hasn't done any dealing. She's great at buying, though. Our basement is stuffed with all sorts of cobwebby lamps and grimy chairs.

"Well, I'm busy, too," I say. "Tanna and I have *lots* of things going on."

The Claw scrunches up her eyebrows and her face turns redder than her nail polish.

"Are any of these activities *organized*?" she asks.

The Claw's big on organized activities, even for adults. She and my dad belong to a book group, a supper club, some sort of ballroom dance troupe, and a weekly "go green" discussion group. I think that group's sort of fallen apart though, since at the last meeting one of the couples admitted they don't recycle.

Even so, the Claw's got my dad pretty "organized."

Before the Claw, I didn't even know that adults could sign up for clubs like that. It makes sense, I guess. I just never really thought about it. Why would I have? My dad used to come home from work every night and watch *Hardball* and ESPN.

Maybe this is bad, but I'm not that interested in organized activities. I took ballet until the second grade, but then my

dad forgot to sign me up for third grade, so I stopped going. I didn't even notice until around Christmas, when our housekeeper used one of my slippers as a potholder.

I sometimes help Mr. Schopper, the drama teacher, paint scenery for school plays. But that's not because I like drama or even art. I just like Mr. Schopper. He and my mom and dad all went to college together and he still keeps a picture of her up in his house. He told me that once, even though I haven't seen it. I've never been to his house before.

The only other thing I do on a regular basis—besides my homework—is help Tanna try to read the future.

But since I don't think the Claw would count that as an organized activity, I settle for a nod instead.

The Claw smiles sweetly and lifts her champagne. "Cheers!" she says. She clinks with my dad, then knocks my water glass lightly.

I lean back in my chair, surprised to have won the argument so easily. Maybe the Claw's suffering from that *Bridezilla* syndrome Tanna warned me about. She learned about it from this TV show where all these brides-to-be go crazy planning their weddings. They have really awful mood

swings and the littlest problem—the wrong tablecloth or a bad hairstyle—can totally set them off. *Whoa.* If the Claw's a Bridezilla *now*, she'll probably have scales and breathe fire by October.

On the other hand, October is really far away.

Chapter 3

If there's anything more disgusting than a boy eating lunch, I don't want to know about it. Seriously. If you ask me, a sixth-grade boy eating a simple sandwich is way scarier than *Saw* and *Hostel* combined.

For instance, right now I'm sitting in the cafeteria listening to Max Dreyfuss burp his way through the *Simpsons* theme song.

The whole table—except me—totally cracks up. I rewrap my sandwich and stick it back in my bag. I've completely lost my appetite. If I get hungry later, I'll just eat in the bathroom.

Last year this never would have happened. In the fifth grade there was no such thing as a coed lunch. It wasn't a rule or anything, but the tables just sort of naturally fell all girl, all boy.

I glance around the cafeteria. There are still a few all-girl tables here and there. If it were up to me, I'd be sitting at one right now. But Tanna always picks where we eat and she thinks Max and his friends are hilarious.

Sixth grade is a lot different from fifth grade, in good and bad ways. Like this year we actually switch classrooms for every subject instead of staying in one place all day. If you ask me, that's a good thing, since last year Mrs. Aimes was my teacher and I wasn't all that crazy about her. She smelled like VapoRub and said weird things like, "Fiddlesticks!" whenever she got angry.

But this year the kids have changed, too. Not that they're actually different kids. I've known most of them practically my whole life. My school, Churchill Academy, goes from pre-K up to twelfth grade and my class has a lot of lifers in it. That's Churchill-speak for students who've been there since nursery school. Being a lifer doesn't really mean much, except you get to be in this big yearbook photo when you graduate. Since I didn't start Churchill until kindergarten, I'm not technically a lifer. Even if I stay until twelfth grade, I'll always be a year off. It's sort of annoying, since preschool and kindergarten are pretty much the same thing. I mean, unless you're actually in preschool or kindergarten, who can really tell the difference between the two?

"Hey, we just got a plasma screen," Evan Bender announces as he shoves half a turkey sandwich into his mouth. "Anyone want to come over and watch?" As he talks, little pieces of meat and bread shoot out across the table.

"Yuck! I already showered once today!" Tanna shrieks, moving away from Evan and out of the line of fire. "Next time try keeping the food *inside* your mouth."

Evan's cheeks turn light pink as everyone cracks up again.

"I'm in," Gus Whitman says, turning to Tanna. "Even though we got two for Christmas."

Tanna thinks Gus is the cutest boy in our grade, but I have no idea what she's talking about. His blue eyes are so droopy, he always looks like he's about to fall asleep, and I don't think he's ever brushed his hair. Not once.

"How 'bout you?" Gus is asking Tanna. "Wanna go?"

Tanna flips her hair and smiles. "Can't. I have to babysit my brothers."

I turn to her, surprised. Tanna does have three little brothers, but she doesn't watch them all that often. The twins, Ryter and Alex, are only one and a half and are kind of a handful. And Tanna's other little brother, Milo, is eight, but he's a major pain. All he and Tanna ever do is fight. Her mom usually only has her babysit when there's some sort of emergency and she can't find a sitter.

Before I can ask her about it, though, Evan turns to me.

"How about you, Molly? Wanna come over?"

Evan lives down the street from me. I pass his house at least twice a day, going to and from school. And every Christmas his parents set up this huge, really cute inflatable snowman in their front yard.

Even so, the thought of hanging out there makes my stomach do this weird accordion thing and I feel sort of nauseous.

I open my mouth to say I-have-no-idea-what when Sophie Kravitz and her best friends, Anne Rankin and Tessa Wright, slide in at the very end of our table.

"Hi, Gus," Sophie says, ignoring everyone else. It's weird the way she doesn't even bother to hide the fact that she likes him. They're both in Social Studies with me and Sophie's always leaning over Gus's desk, asking him stupid questions like, "Is Antarctica *really* a continent?" and "What's the difference between latitude and longitude again?"

At first I thought Sophie was just dumb, but last test Mr. Richards announced that she has the highest average in the whole class, so obviously she isn't that dumb.

I only have an eighty-two and even I know the difference between latitude and longitude.

"Hey." Gus nods, staring down at his Sun Chips. I've noticed that his voice doesn't sound very friendly when he talks to her.

Sophie snaps open her bag, which is white patent leather and looks way too fancy for school. I've been carrying the same knapsack since the second grade, which I like just fine. It's got a lot of pockets.

Still, staring at Sophie's bag, my stomach does that weird accordion stretch again.

I watch as she pulls out a Red Bull and tries to hand it to

Gus. As she extends her arm the stack of gold bracelets on her wrist jingle.

"Want one?" she asks. "I brought extra."

"Uh, no thanks."

Tanna nudges me and rolls her eyes. Sophie really bugs her. I think it's because she's jealous of all the attention she gets, but I'd never say that to her. And Tanna would never admit it anyway.

Sophie's new to Churchill—her family moved from North Carolina to New Jersey over the summer—though the way she flounces around, you'd never know it. Ever since school started, she's been a really big deal. Tanna says it's because people up North are suckers for a Southern accent, but I think it's because Sophie looks so sophisticated. The white bag is only part of it. I overheard her telling Anne once that she gets her long chestnut hair professionally straightened and it takes almost six hours. She basically has to clear out an entire Saturday every four months. Plus, she's the only person in my class who has an iPhone. Most of the kids, including me, don't even have cell phones yet.

"I'll take that," Max Dreyfuss burps to Sophie, who wrinkles up her nose. I can tell she's grossed out, but when she sees that Gus is cracking up, she forces a laugh and passes the can down the table.

Tanna smooshes her lunch bag into a ball and stands. I get up, too, but as I move the sole of my tennis shoe rubs against the bench and makes this really loud, low farting noise.

That did *not* just happen.

Everyone at the table looks at me. Their stares are enough to trigger an instant sneaker-fart replay in my head.

Yep. It happened.

"It wasn't me!" I cry, but my voice is swallowed up by all of the *Ewwws* and *No ways*.

Max Dreyfuss wrinkles up his nose, disgusted. *Great.* The human burp-box thinks that *I'm* gross.

I watch as Sophie types something into her iPhone, then passes it to Tessa and Anne (like me, they're both cell-less). The three girls look my way and giggle. This time, Sophie's laughter sounds genuine.

"Oh, grow up," Tanna shouts down the table. She flips her hair and places her arm protectively around my shoulder. "Ready?"

"Thanks," I whisper as we walk away from the group.

How great is my best friend? I mean, I just totally humiliated myself in the worst possible way, and she doesn't even blink. She really is the best.

As soon as we're a safe distance away from the table, Tanna stops and looks at me. She's got this really worried look on her face and her eyebrows are practically touching.

"Maybe you should stop eating vegetables," she suggests.

"Wait, what?"

"Vegetables give you gas, Molly. Didn't you know that?"

"Ew! I don't have gas. That was my *shoe*!"

"Or maybe you're drinking too much soda?"

I raise my hand, totally annoyed. "I told you. It wasn't me. It was my—"

"Don't get mad. I'm only trying to help," Tanna says, shaking her head.

That's another thing about this year: Tanna won't stop giving me advice. Almost every day, she's got some sort of helpful tip, like how leggings are much cooler than tights or that walking with my shoulders back will make me look taller.

I know she's only trying to help, but all that advice gets sort of annoying. Especially since I never ask for it.

"I'm not mad," I say. We start to walk again, weaving through the cafeteria and out toward the yard. "But I didn't *do* anything. That was my foot."

Tanna sighs. "Libras *so* hate conflict." She pats the secret pocket in her coat. "Hey, let's check the cards. They'll warn us if anything else really bad is going to happen today."

I shake my head. "I've got to finish my Algebra worksheet."

"Fine. After school, then?"

"I thought you had to babysit."

"No way. I just said that. My mom would *never* let me hang out at Evan's." Tanna glances back at our table and her eyes narrow. Sophie's sitting directly across from Gus now, in Tanna's empty seat.

I have no idea why Tanna couldn't just tell everyone the truth about Evan's house. But I'm definitely not asking for an explanation.

Like I said, things are different this year.

Chapter 4

THE REST OF my day goes from bad to worse to even worse. For starters, every time Max Dreyfuss sees me now, he tucks his hand under his armpit and makes those gross fart noises.

Unfortunately, Max sees me a lot. We're in almost every class together.

And we started playing basketball in PE. At first I was relieved, because that meant softball was finally over—and softball was pretty painful (why do they even call them *soft*-balls anyway? Believe me, there's nothing soft about them). I always got stuck playing catcher and the equipment was way too big. The only time I even came close to catching the ball was when it got lost inside my uniform.

Basketballs are a lot bigger than softballs, so I figured I had a much better chance of catching one. Besides, my dad's like a total basketball freak. We've been watching Nets games together since I could talk. And to be honest, it never looked all that complicated. I really thought I'd be a natural.

Wow, was I wrong. There's a big difference between watching a sport and actually playing it. Like when the ball accidentally rolled my way during the game, I grabbed it and took off. Sure I *knew* about dribbling. But with an entire gym class chasing after you, who has the time? And Mrs. Sixsmith only made things worse, blowing her whistle in my face and screaming, *"Traveling!"* like I was under arrest or something. That's when I panicked and ran off of the court completely.

At least PE is an all-girl class. If Max Dreyfuss and his armpit farts had been there, I'd *definitely* have had a nervous breakdown.

Class is finally over now, but Mrs. Sixsmith is making me stay after—again—to practice my dribbling. She won't shut up about how dribbling is an essential part of basketball, but it's, like, *Duh!* I already know that. I just forgot.

At least I'm not alone. Mrs. Sixsmith said her sciatica was acting up, so she asked Julie Wolff to stay, too, to demonstrate the perfect dribble.

Julie's quiet and sort of keeps to herself. During our other classes, I hardly know she's there. But in PE she's a total star. She's definitely one of the best athletes in my grade. She even outscores the boys' class when we play them.

I think Mrs. Sixsmith wants to adopt her.

I'm a little worried Julie will be mad at me because she has to stay late, but she's actually nice about it and even offers a few pointers.

"When you dribble the ball, imagine it's the head of someone you *really* hate," she suggests. "Don't be afraid to pound."

I close my eyes and picture Max Dreyfuss's face, then bounce the ball really hard and try to slap it with my hand. I miss. Completely.

Smack!

The ball hits me in the chin and rolls away.

"Omigosh, are you okay?" Julie rushes over. "I'm so sorry!"

I rub my face. "No, it's fine. It didn't hurt," I lie, because the pain doesn't really bother me. I'm way too relieved that the rest of the class is gone to even care about a broken jaw.

Mrs. Sixsmith checks my face and counts my teeth. "Uh, I think that's all for today, girls." She places a hand over her heart and gives me a your-klutziness-might-just-kill-me sort of look.

"I guess I'm just hopeless when it comes to sports," I tell Julie as we walk back to the locker room.

She giggles. "I don't know. I think opening your eyes when you play might really improve your game."

"Ooops." I steal a look at Julie. Her body's sort of blocky and she's more than a whole head taller than I am. She always wears sweats and her jet-black hair is cut in a sporty, chin-length bob that she parts on the side and keeps off of her face with a headband.

Tanna says Julie is really unfashionable, but I think she looks just fine.

"You're amazing at sports," I tell her, then immediately feel stupid for saying something so obvious.

Julie doesn't seem to notice, though. "My whole family is," she says lightly. "My dad was an all-American lacrosse player when he was in college and my mom almost went to the Olympics for diving."

"Wow." I don't want the conversation to end, but what else can I say? My dad really likes the Nets?

Julie shrugs. "It's not such a big deal. Everyone's good at something."

I nod but I'm not so sure I agree. What am I good at?

"Listen," Julie says slowly. "If you want, I'll help you. All you need is a little practice. Maybe during recess?" Her eyes flicker over to me. "I mean, unless you're too busy . . ."

I smile. "No that'd be great. Thanks."

Julie smiles back as the pink rushes into her face, staining her cheeks.

By the time I leave the locker room, I'm feeling a little better. But when I meet Tanna after school, everything falls apart. Again.

As soon as she sees me, she screams. "Ew! What happened to your face?"

"Ha-ha," I answer. "Very funny."

"I'm serious, Molly. Look." Tanna opens her locker and points at the oval mirror she's pasted inside the door, right above her heart-shaped picture of Nick Jonas (another boy she thinks is gorgeous and I could totally care less about).

I peer at my reflection. My entire chin is bruised. It looks like a red-and-blue highlighter exploded all over my jaw.

"I, uh, had sort of an accident in PE," I explain. I can't stop staring at myself. It's definitely gross looking. But it's also sort of cool, the way all the colors swirl together like tie-dye.

"PE? That was *hours* ago," Tanna says. "How long have you been walking around like that? Do you think anyone noticed?"

"It doesn't really hurt," I mutter. "But thanks for asking."

Tanna frowns. "I'm sorry. Are you sure you're okay?"

"It's fine," I say, shifting my jaw back and forth. "I can't feel anything."

"Good. I know just what to do, don't worry." She grabs her bag and slams her locker door shut. "We'll go to Rite Aid and buy some cover-up."

"No. No makeup," I say. I hate makeup. It itches my face

and I always end up smearing it. Plus, it makes me feel weird, like I'm four years old, playing dress-up.

Tanna sighs. "Molly, this is an emergency. You can't walk around like that. You're hideous."

"Hey!"

I touch my chin, suddenly self-conscious. *Great. Like the sneaker fart and the basketball disaster weren't enough. Now I'm maimed for life.*

Tanna rests her hand on my arm. "I'm sorry. I'm only trying to help." She smiles at me. "Okay, how about this? We'll just go back to your house and ice it. Maybe the swelling will be gone by tomorrow morning."

"Good idea," I say. I feel calmer already. Tanna has this way of saying things; you just know it's going to be okay.

Only it isn't.

When we get home, the Claw is waiting for us. She's so excited, she doesn't even notice my chin.

"I've got a surprise for you, girls!" she cries, ushering us to the basement.

My stomach flip-flops. Something tells me this isn't a good kind of surprise.

I look around, trying to remember the last time I was in the basement. It used to be my playroom when I was little, but over the years it's sort of morphed into a storage space. When the Claw moved in she made my dad clear it out to make room for her antiques, but it still looks pretty much the same. The only difference is that now her junk is all over the place instead of his.

"Isn't this cute?" the Claw says, pointing to a corner of the room where a little table is stacked with all sorts of beads, paints, and construction paper. It looks like the arts-and-crafts center in a second-grade classroom.

"Isn't it just fabulous?" the Claw crows again.

Tanna raises her eyebrows.

"I don't get it," I say.

The Claw smiles another total nonsmile. "I thought this would be the perfect compromise. It'll lend some structure to your after-school time." She moves toward the stairs. "And this way, I won't have to worry about you."

"But you don't ever worry about me," I blurt out, then instantly regret it. I really wish there was a remote control for conversations. I'd definitely use the rewind and delete buttons. A lot.

The Claw freezes, then turns slowly back around. This time she doesn't even bother with the pseudo-smile.

"This is a big year for me, Molly," she says. Her voice is soft but sharper than her nails. "I want my wedding to be perfect. And I can't have you hanging around upstairs while I'm trying to plan. So this is your new headquarters, got it?"

Tanna squares off her shoulders. "You're sticking us in the basement? I don't think so."

"Well, if you don't like the new rules, then *you*, my dear, can go home." The Claw claps her hands together. "Now. Why don't you girls break open those watercolors? I've got a wedding to plan." She heads for the door, then glances back at me over her shoulder. "And wash your face, okay, Molly? You're a mess."

Tanna and I listen to her click away, then look at each other, incredulous.

"She's such a witch," I say, swallowing the tears in my throat.

"Totally heinous," Tanna agrees. And then, in a tiny voice, she adds, "I'm really sorry, Molly."

I stare at my feet. If I open my mouth right now, I'll start to cry.

"You could always call your dad and complain," Tanna suggests.

That's true, I could. But just the memory of the Claw's voice makes my skin prickle. Do I really want to make her mad? Plus, my dad was on *her* side last night at dinner. I don't see how that'll have changed overnight.

I shake my head and Tanna doesn't push. She watches me for a minute to make sure I'm okay, then looks around the basement and snorts. "So what now?"

"Wanna go to your house?"

Tanna groans. "I've got one word for you: Mi-lo."

I lean against the edge of the table and nod, knowing Tanna's right. You'd think her twin brothers—the one-year-olds—would be the reason we never hang out at her house, but Milo's the real problem. He's a total pest. No matter what we're doing, he wants to do it, too. We could be painting our toenails or braiding our hair and he'd still insist on joining us. And when we refuse, he tattles to Mrs. Walker, who says something really lame like, "The more the merrier, girls" and we have to include him. And then the whole day is ruined.

"Fine," I say. "So what do *you* want to do?"

"Oh! I know!" Tanna says. She grabs a piece of construction paper and folds it on a diagonal.

"Um, what's that?" I ask, even though I already know the answer.

"Cootie-catcher time," Tanna sings as she trims the edge. "You can make one, too."

Cootie-catchers are these origami fortune-tellers Tanna's babysitter showed us how to make. It's actually pretty easy—all you do is fold a piece of paper into a bunch of triangles, draw different colored dots and numbers on each side, and write some fortunes under the flaps. But they're also pretty boring. I keep waiting for Tanna to get sick of them, but so far she hasn't, and she's probably gone through three reams of paper making them.

I sigh and grab a piece of yellow paper, making all the folds and cuts in about three minutes. But when I try to think up fortunes I get sort of stuck. I want them all to be happy, but a little surprising, too. Not the usual "You'll be famous" sort of thing. And definitely nothing about secret admirers.

I'm still trying to choose when Tanna finishes her cootie-catcher and slips her fingers into the flaps.

"Pick a color," she tells me.

I stare down at the little paper pyramid covering her hands. "Blue," I say, pointing at the dot.

Tanna's fingers move back and forth, flapping the pyramid up, down, and side-to-side. "B-L-U-E. Okay, now pick a number."

"Five," I choose, since it's the lowest number.

The fortune-teller flips open and closed as Tanna counts. "Now pick another number."

"Five," I repeat, trying not to yawn.

Tanna scowls at me like she knows I'm not trying as hard as I should but doesn't say anything. She lifts up the flap of paper with the number five written on top.

"Watch out for vampires," she reads.

I glare at her. "That's not a fortune."

"It is so." Tanna lowers the cootie-catcher and shakes out her hair. "Think about it, Molly. You live with the Claw."

"So? What's that supposed to mean?"

Tanna shoots me a *Puh-lease!* sort of look. "Well, you have to admit. She's a total vampire. I don't think the fortune's so off-base."

I know this is a stupid thing to get mad about, but I can't

help it. *I* was trying to write nice fortunes only. Why did Tanna have to be so harsh? I stare down at my unfinished cootie-catcher and wait for the mood to pass.

"Forget it," Tanna says. Her voice is a little too bright and I can tell she's trying to make up for the bad fortune. "We could play MASH."

MASH is another one of Tanna's favorite activities. It's this game where you write the letters—they stand for Mansion, Apartment, Shack, House—at the top of a piece of paper, along with a list of four boys, four types of vehicles, and four different careers. Then you pick a number and start to count, crossing off the choices every time you reach the number. What you're left with is supposed to be your future.

According to my last round of MASH, I'm going to marry SpongeBob SquarePants and live in a shack with 730 kids.

For obvious reasons, I'm not so eager to play again.

I wrinkle my nose. "Pass."

Tanna straightens and walks deliberately away from the arts-and-crafts table. "Hey! I know what we can do down here!"

"What?"

"Duh! Go through the Claw's stuff." She grabs a bright

red lamp with a gold lampshade trimmed in black velvet braid. "You couldn't pay me to put this in my house."

I chew my lower lip. If we break anything we are—or at least I am—dead. "Uh, be careful okay? That stuff's really old."

Tanna unfolds an ancient-looking stepladder and blows on a busted rung. Little speckles of brown dust shoot into the air and flutter around the room. "Oh, I'll be gentle. Come on, help me look."

I glance at the arts-and-crafts table. The Claw didn't even spring for *Crayola* markers—she bought the drugstore brand instead. How lame is that?

"Fine," I say. "But we have to put everything back when we're done."

Ten minutes and about four hundred dust bunnies later I'm about to pass out. I'm covered in gook and all we've found so far is a creaky old chair that's way too fragile to sit on and a dresser with a zillion drawers so small they couldn't hold anything except for maybe a few stamps.

"No wonder the Claw isn't working," Tanna says, wrinkling her nose. "Her stuff stinks."

And that's when I see it.

"Look," I point. "On top of the mini-sofa."

Tanna frowns. "It's called a love seat, Molly."

"Whatever. I think I found a TV!"

Tanna's gaze follows my finger, toward the big wooden cube with the supersmall screen that's practically kissing the water meter. There's a long green electric cord hanging off the back.

"I seriously doubt this gets cable," Tanna says as we pull it down to the floor. "But it's better than painting. Maybe we can catch *Days of Our Lives*."

We crumple up some construction paper and try to wipe off the grime.

"Yuck," Tanna says, holding up a black sheet of paper that used to be green. "I'll bet this thing hasn't been washed in *centuries*."

I run my dusting paper down the side of the box, feeling the cracks and dents in the dark brown wood. There's an on/off switch under the rectangular screen, a bright red dial, and four rows of tiny gold buttons, each with a different letter stamped on top. It's a keyboard, I realize, only not like the one on a computer. These look more old-fashioned, like they were taken from some sort of weird antique typewriter.

My hand floats across the buttons, which make a cool

clicking noise as they're pushed. Tanna stands next to me, studying the machine.

"It sure is ugly," she says.

"I don't know," I say, stepping back. "I think it's sort of cool looking."

"Maybe it's an old video game," she suggests. "My dad has something called Intellivision in our garage."

I grab the cord and plug the machine into the wall. Tanna switches it on. Nothing happens.

"It's broken," she says. "Bummer."

"Let me try," I say, surprising myself. Tanna's a lot better with computers than I am. I don't even like to play video games all that much. They make me sort of nervous.

I walk over and flick the on/off button.

This time the machine wakes up. The monitor glows a bright white and two silver bells dance in from opposite sides of the screen.

I can't remember the last time I could do something Tanna couldn't. I have to admit, it feels pretty good. Not in a braggy sort of way, though. Just sweet.

"How'd you do that?" she asks. She's staring at me now, a baffled expression on her face.

Since I have absolutely no idea, I don't answer her. Besides, she doesn't have to look *so* shocked.

The bells are swept away, replaced by a flowery script that reads *Tell Me Who?* and then a command: *Enter Name.*

"I guess it is a video game," I say.

"Well the graphics on Wii are a lot better." There's a tiny pout on Tanna's face and I can tell she's still sore about not being able to work the machine. "And it doesn't even let you enter two players."

"Maybe the old games weren't two-player," I point out, trying to be positive. This is the only thing separating me from another round of MASH. I wave Tanna toward the box. "You go first."

Tanna taps the keys, spelling out her name: Stephanie Rose Walker.

Nothing happens.

She scowls. "I told you it's broken."

I step forward and start typing. Letters instantly appear onscreen and I try to hide my smile.

Tanna gets all quiet and folds her arms across her chest. She has a funny look on her face, but I can't tell if she's mad or just surprised again.

"Maybe it was stuck," I mumble, twisting the red dial.

Tanna opens her mouth, when all of a sudden the machine starts to shake. Squiggly lines and dots—I don't know if it's static or an actual part of the game—crowd the monitor. We wait for a car, Mario, or some sort of intruder to appear so Tanna can start driving, jumping, or shooting.

But nothing happens.

Tanna tosses up her hands. "What a piece of . . ."

She trails off as the screen clears. The flowery script is back.

It reads:

BRIDE 💍 *Stephanie Rose Walker*
GROOM 🎀 *Sir Edmund Alistair Blake*

As the words appear, music floats up from the machine. And that's when my legs go all weak and melty.

The tune is totally warped and sounds really bad, but I know this song.

Everyone knows this song.

It's the "Wedding March."

Chapter 5

THE SCREEN IS dark again. Tanna and I are staring at it, and I think we're both too freaked out to move.

"Whoa," Tanna breathes, finally breaking the silence. "Is that, I mean, do you think . . ."

"I-I don't know what this is," I say. My words come out all strangled and breathy.

"Who's Sir Edmund Alistair Blake?" Tanna asks, still staring at the blank screen. Her eyes are so wide, they look like bright blue fried eggs. "What kind of name is *Edmund* anyway? What's he doing in your basement?"

"I don't know," I say again. My chest feels tight.

Get a grip, I tell myself. I think of the Claw and, for the first time ever, that actually helps me relax. Only the Claw would buy such a weird, totally unfun game.

And that's what this is. Just a game.

"Let's put it away," I hear myself say. My voice still sounds strange. "This is boring. All it does is match people up with random names."

"Maybe they're not so random." Tanna tears her gaze away from the box and looks at me. Her cheeks are bright red. "Maybe the machine knows what it's talking about."

I try to make myself laugh, but the sound that comes out is a sort of half-gasp/half-snort. "Tanna, come on. It's a total piece of junk. You said so yourself."

"I don't know . . . I might be having second thoughts." Tanna fiddles with the control panel. When nothing happens her mouth tightens and she turns to me. "You should try."

I chew my lip. I have a bad feeling about this. A really bad feeling. But what am I supposed to do? Convince Tanna to put the machine away and help me make a collage? There's just no way.

So I step forward and enter my name: Molly Ryan Paige. I don't look at Tanna as I type, but I can feel her standing next

to me, staring. I close my eyes and twist the red button. Pride skips through me, but this time it only lasts a few seconds.

The machine trembles and the same warbled "Wedding March" seeps into the room. That's when Tanna gasps.

My eyes pop open and I look at the screen. I can't believe what I'm reading:

BRIDE 💍 *Molly Ryan Paige*
GROOM 🎀 *Glenn Aaron Borack*

"No way!" Tanna shrieks.

I open my mouth, then close it. Then I open it again. I'm in such total shock that I can't even say the one simple word that keeps blipping through my head.

Yuck. Yuck. Yuck Yuck Yuck Yuck *Yuck.*

Here's the thing: I *know* Glenn (Aaron) Borack. He lives in my neighborhood; he's on my bus and his parents are in book group with my dad and the Claw. He's short—really short—with dark hair that never looks clean.

But wait. It gets worse.

Glenn Borack is in the fifth grade. He's a grade *below* me in school. *Glenn Borack is a whole year younger than I am.*

He's practically Milo's age. Okay, maybe he's not that little, but whatever. Younger is younger. Plus, he brings these really stinky sandwiches for lunch and they totally smell up the cafeteria. He's the only person I've ever met who actually eats liverwurst. *Happily*.

I clear my throat. "This doesn't mean anything," I stammer. "I mean, we don't even know what the machine is for."

"You might be right," Tanna says. "Try someone else."

She's got a point. If I can prove that the machine is a phony, then I'm off the hook.

This time I work fast, inputting the names of people who are already married. My Grandma Sylvie. Tanna's Aunt Liza. Mrs. Sixsmith.

And the machine never misses. Not once. At least I don't think it does. Mrs. Sixsmith probably wasn't the best test, since I really have no idea who her husband is.

But the machine is definitely right about everyone else.

I input Tanna's mom and her dad's name—Douglas McAdams Walker—flashes across the screen, even though everyone calls him Mac.

"That's amazing," Tanna marvels. "How could it know something like that?"

Is it my imagination or does she actually sound *happy* about all of this? I lift my hand to try again when Tanna stops me.

"Enough," she says. "I'm totally convinced."

I frown. "About what?"

Tanna rolls her eyes. "What do you mean 'about what'? Don't you see what this is?"

I bunch my fists into tiny balls. *Don't say it. Don't say it. Don't say it.*

"*This* is a marriage machine," Tanna explains. She points at the water meter and giggles. "It's a marriage meter."

I can't believe she's laughing. I'm stuck marrying a stupid fifth-grader and my best friend thinks it's hilarious. As far as I'm concerned, there is absolutely *nothing* funny about Glenn Aaron Borack.

"Don't you get it?" she continues. "The *who* in *Tell Me Who?* is your future husband or wife." She smiles. "It's a Who-Meter."

Omigod, my life is OVER.

I shake my head. "It can't be," I insist. "There's no such thing."

"This is *huge*," Tanna rushes on. "So much better than numerology or tarot cards or *anything*. I mean, do you know what this means?" She pauses. "Okay, I'm not really sure what this means, but it has to be amazing." She looks at me, her eyebrows arched. "I wonder why it only works for *you*, though. That doesn't make sense at all."

"Wait a minute." I know I should be insulted, but at the moment I'm too freaked out to care. I will *not* accept this. Glenn Borack has absolutely nothing to do with me, or my future. He's just a smelly-sandwich–eating boy. "Why are you so happy? I thought you weren't even *going* to get married?"

Tanna's always wanted to be a journalist and anchor the evening news. She plans to replace Katie Couric after she graduates from college.

"I'll do both," she says, shrugging. "I mean, the news only lasts an hour."

"I don't know," I say. "I'm sure there's another explanation." I'm trying really hard to speak in a slow, calm voice. But it's hard. Really, really hard. Because inside my head, I can't stop thinking, *Glenn Borack? Is the Who-Meter crazy? Is it totally short-circuiting? I am* not *marrying him.*

Maybe Tanna has it wrong. Maybe it's not a marriage machine after all. Maybe it's like a—

Glenn Borack? No way. I'd rather become a priest—okay, a nun. I'm Jewish, but whatever. I'll make it work.

Tanna shakes her head. "It's definitely a marriage meter. What else would it be?" She turns to me. "I know. Try your dad's name. After all, he and the Claw are getting married!"

Okay, I admit it. I purposely didn't try my dad's name before. I'm a total wimp.

But Tanna's right. My father's engaged and I can't think of a better test.

I hold my breath as I type in the letters and turn the dial. My father's name—*Mitchell Simon Paige*—appears onscreen.

Maybe the Claw's name won't show up, I think, crossing my fingers. I'm so confused.

I stare at the Who-Meter as a name flashes across the monitor: *Rachel Ann Ryan.*

Well, that doesn't exactly help my side of the argument, but it does make sense. Rachel Ann Ryan is my mom. She was, after all, my dad's wife.

Here's the thing, though: even though she died of cancer when I was in the second grade, Rachel Ann Ryan's still my

mom. So I really don't see how the situation is any different for my dad. Technically she's still his wife.

So then what's the Claw's toothbrush doing in his bathroom?

The Who-Meter interrupts me. It's totally melting down. The screen's filled with that weird confetti static and it's shaking all over.

"Maybe I killed it," I say, hopefully.

And then the Claw's name—*Phyllis Eileen Kruft*—creeps across the screen.

The tiny smile on my face does a backbend.

So that's that, I think. The wedding's real. It's happening. And the Claw's here to stay.

"Molly, I'm really sorry," Tanna says. She's trying hard to look sympathetic, but her eyes are supershiny and her cheeks are red. I can tell she's secretly happy that the Who-Meter works.

Of course she is. She gets to marry a Sir.

I let my hands fall to my sides. My arms feel like barbells. This is the worst day ever.

On the other hand, if I'm marrying Glenn Aaron Borack, things will definitely be getting a whole lot worse.

Chapter 6

I'M GOING TO kill Tanna. Seriously. *Kill.*

Last night she *promised* not to say a word about the whole Glenn Borack situation to anyone.

"Honestly, Molly," she said about twenty times. "You don't even have to ask."

And then what does she go and do? The minute Glenn gets on the bus this morning she shouts—and I mean *shouts*—"Hi, Glenn!" and ducks behind the seat.

So of course, because I was sitting next to her and was way too horrified to move, Glenn thought *I* was the one saying hi.

He looked especially loserish, too. He was eating some sort of disgusting egg sandwich and his face was covered with ketchup. And he was wearing green. All green. A rumply green turtleneck and wrinkled green pants. Even his tube socks were green—I checked.

It was, I decided, the perfect color for him. Lots of disgusting things are green. Like mold. And boogers.

My cheeks were so hot I'm surprised the Frizz didn't burst into flames.

I scowled at Glenn. He made one of those obnoxious oooh-I'm-so-scared faces and turned back around.

It might not have been all that bad, except that Max Dreyfuss was sitting behind us and saw the whole thing. He laughed so hard, he started to snort, then fell off his seat and into the aisle.

So now, when Max isn't making armpit farts at me he just shouts "Hi, Glenn!" and totally cracks up.

It's lunch now and I'm still fuming.

"Calm down," Tanna says as we carry our trays through the cafeteria. "It was just a joke."

"Well, it was really, *really* hilarious," I say. "I can't believe you did that. You promised."

"I promised not to tell anyone about you and Glenn. And I didn't, did I?"

The words *you and Glenn* make my spine feel all quivery.

"That's so not the point and you know it," I say.

"Look, I'm sorry," Tanna says. "I was *kidding*. I won't do it again." She steers us to a small table in the corner, way across the room from the usual crowd.

"Don't you want to eat with everyone else?" I ask. I rest my tray on the table but can't bring myself to sit. It's not that I actually want to eat with Max and his armpit farts, but there's safety in numbers. Tanna would never mention the Who-Meter in front of those guys.

And I really don't want to talk about the Who-Meter right now. It's been less than twenty-four hours since we found the stupid machine and I already regret it. And not just because of Gross Glenn or the Claw—although they're both pretty awful.

But what's worse—okay, maybe not *worse* but definitely just as bad—is that the Who-Meter is Tanna's latest obsession. She called twice last night after dinner and once this morning before school to talk about it. And she's been passing me notes all day long. I never thought I'd miss tarot cards, but I do.

"We need our privacy," Tanna says. She flips her hair back and glances over at Gus. He's staring at our table with a sort of puzzled look on his face. "Besides, why bother?"

I sink down into a chair and twist open my lemonade. "What do you mean?"

"I Googled Edmund Alistair Blake last night," Tanna says, dropping her voice to a low, excited whisper. "I couldn't really find out that much on him, but there's a ton of stuff about his parents. They're *major*." She dips her grilled cheese sandwich into a little pool of ketchup and nibbles on an end. "I saw this picture of their house, Langley Hall. It's a serious *castle*. Can you believe it, Molly? I'm going to live in England. In a castle."

I frown. I can't help it. It's sort of hard to be happy for your friend's future castle when you're looking at life with Glenn Borack. And what about my MASH prediction? What if that comes true, too? Or some sort of weird MASH/Who-Meter combination?

Omigosh. Glenn Borack and I are going to have 730 kids.

I'd definitely rather be Mrs. SpongeBob SquarePants. At least he's got a good sense of humor. And a job.

I make a serious yuck face and Tanna reaches over to pat my arm.

"Don't worry," she says, reassuringly. "We'll still see each other all the time. I'm sure I'll have a few planes, so I'll be able to visit whenever I want."

My throat feels all stretched and tight. "Listen, maybe we should just forget about yesterday."

Tanna's eyes widen. "Are you crazy? We can't just forget about it."

"Why not?"

"Because the Who-Meter's the best thing that's ever happened to us," Tanna insists, waving her sandwich crust at me. "Do you even realize how much information we're sitting on here? This is a once-in-a-lifetime opportunity."

I look at her. "To do what?"

"I don't know yet," Tanna says, leaning back in her chair. She's got a funny look on her face and I'm not so sure I believe her.

"Well, the machine is in my house and I'm the only one who can work it," I announce. I twist my straw around my finger, but the white band reminds me of a wedding ring, so

I slip it off immediately. "And since I don't think we should use it, I guess—"

"Molly, be smart." Tanna interrupts. "*Everyone* wants to know who they're gonna marry." She waves her hand around, as if she's talking for the entire cafeteria. "And now we can tell them."

"Not true," I tell her as my stomach pulls another squash and stretch. Arguing with Tanna always makes me nervous. "*I* didn't want to know."

Tanna's lips tighten into a hard, straight line. "Come on, you weren't even a tiny bit curious?"

"I wonder where it came from?" I say, to change the subject. I try to make my voice sound playful in a scary sort of way. "I mean, what if the original owner tracks us down and—"

"Forget it," Tanna says, cutting me off. Clearly she isn't in the mood to pretend. "It's been sitting in your basement for months. Before that, it probably sat in someone else's basement. I'll bet the original owner died like a million years ago."

I take a sip of lemonade and look around the room. Julie Wolff is sitting four tables away, with a few of her sporty friends. When I catch her eye she smiles.

Instinctively, my hand shoots up to wave her over.

Tanna watches the exchange and frowns. "What are you doing?"

"Um, Julie's helping me with basketball after lunch." I stand as Julie approaches our table. I'm so relieved I might pass out. For the first time ever, stinking at sports is actually coming in handy.

"Ready to practice?" Julie asks. Her eyes flicker over to Tanna and she smiles shyly. "Great skirt. I love purple."

I turn, noticing Tanna's miniskirt and ruffled top for the first time. Julie's right. They're both really, really purple. But wait . . . since when does Tanna wear purple? That's not an approved Scorpio color. A quick check confirms that her crystals are gone, too.

Tanna flips her hair and looks directly at me. "Did you know that purple's the official color of British royalty?"

"Um, cool," Julie says, obviously confused.

I grab my tray and scrape my chair back. "I'm ready," I tell her. "Just let me dump this and I'll meet you outside, okay?"

"Um, do you want to play, too?" Julie asks Tanna.

"Nah." Tanna opens her bag and pulls out a library book about Princess Diana. "I have some work to do."

Julie and I head outside. I feel sort of bad leaving Tanna alone in the cafeteria. But there's also a part of me that's really relieved she's not joining us. And in a way, that makes me feel even worse.

I'm not sure if they have it at other schools, but there's this club at Churchill called Little Kids Club. It's for the high school students—mostly girls sign up—and they spend recess with different lower school classes, playing games and organizing different activities. Nothing too complicated, mostly things like Simon Says and Red Light Green Light. Still, it's a lot of fun.

Once you hit middle school though, you're on your own. Little Kids Club doesn't bother with you anymore. And you can pretty much do whatever you want during recess so long as you stay on the playground. Personally, I sort of miss the Red Light Green Light days—especially compared to forty straight minutes of basketball practice, which is what I'm stuck doing now.

"Okay, whenever you throw, remember to point your elbows at exactly where you want the ball to go," Julie says.

We're standing in a corner of the playground, between the swing set and the fence. I chose the spot on purpose, since it's more deserted than other places, like the kickball diamond or the picnic tables.

Julie bends her arms, then straightens, releasing the basketball. I watch in awe as it arcs gracefully through the air, bounces off the fence and obediently rolls back to us.

"There's no way I can do that," I tell her. "We might as well skip this part."

"It's really not so hard." Julie hands me the ball. "Just give it a try."

"Seriously, can't you just teach me how to fake the whole game? Isn't there a way I can look like I'm playing without actually having to touch the ball?"

Julie folds her arms over her chest. "No way."

"Why not?"

"Because you really *can* play, Molly. You just need to psych yourself up. If you tell yourself you're terrible at something, you will be."

I'm not so sure it's that simple, but I keep my doubts to myself. I scan the playground, noticing that Sophie, Tessa, and Anne are just a few feet away, standing in front of the swing set. They're all huddled around Sophie's iPhone, giggling.

Great. Why'd they have to hang out there, of all places? Even though they're not paying any attention to me I'd still feel a whole lot better if they were somewhere else. Alaska would be nice.

I turn my back to the group. "Maybe you should show me one more time?"

Julie smiles. "Quit stalling. And remember—keep your eyes open this time."

I take the ball and pull it toward my chest, training my elbows on the fence. Pushing my arms out forcefully, I release.

Hey! That actually felt pretty good! I smile as I wait for the ball to smack against the metal.

Behind me, I hear a loud *thwack!* followed by a long and painful scraping sound.

"My phone!"

Julie makes a face. "Uh-oh."

I turn. The basketball is bouncing down the playground, Sophie's iPhone skidding behind it. The two sort of look like they're playing tag.

Anne breaks away from the group to chase down the phone.

I'm so dead.

My stomach knots up as Sophie huffs her way over to me. "If it's broken, you owe me six hundred dollars," she announces.

"I-I'm really sorry," I say. The playground's totally silent now. I can feel everyone watching me. "I'll pay you back."

"It was an accident," Julie adds.

Sophie rolls her eyes. "Do you even *have* six hundred dollars?" she asks me.

"I don't—I mean, no. But if you want me to call my dad—"

"I think it's okay," Anne says, rushing up to us. She hands Sophie the phone and shoots me this really poisonous look.

Still, I feel like hugging her.

Sophie touches the screen. "It's scratched," she announces. She glares at me, her face pinched and angry. "If I've lost one picture, you're in serious trouble."

She storms off with Tessa and Anne on either side, their arms draped over her shoulders reassuringly.

"Whoa," Julie says. "Are you okay?"

I try to smile, but it's hard. My heart is hammering and my legs feel like spaghetti. "Yeah. Thanks for trying to help."

Julie shrugs. "Personally, I don't see why any kid needs a six-hundred dollar phone." She tilts her head to one side thoughtfully. "Except maybe Miley Cyrus."

I smile at her, grateful for the distraction. "How about the kids from *High School Musical*?"

Julie shakes her head. "They don't count, because they're not really kids. Did you know that? They're all, like, twenty-five. Isn't that weird?"

I giggle, but my heart isn't really in it. My brain's still stuck on Sophie Kravitz hating me, which is totally ridiculous. Because I know deep down that Julie's right. And I know that if I were Tanna, I would've stood up for myself. If I were Tanna, I wouldn't care about stupid Sophie or her stupid phone. Not one bit.

But here's the thing: I'm not Tanna. And I'm not Julie either.

I'm me. And I care. I just can't help it.

Chapter 7

Before the Claw, Nets games were a really big thing for my dad and me. We'd pop a huge vat of popcorn and wear these matching jerseys—number five, for Jason Kidd. Then we'd pile into the den, plop ourselves down onto the couch, and try to watch the whole game straight through, without getting up once—not even to go to the bathroom or get more popcorn. I'm not really sure how that last rule got started, but for some reason we decided it was bad luck to leave early.

I know it sounds sort of uncomfortable, but it was actually a lot of fun.

And then the Claw came along.

My dad and I still watch the games together, but it's really not the same. First of all, the Claw won't let us pop popcorn since she says the smell stinks up the house. And whenever we cheer or shout at the TV she complains about the noise, so we have to keep it down. Plus, she always interrupts at the absolute worst times—like when there's only ten seconds left on the clock.

We've sort of forgotten about the matching jerseys, too, though I guess that's not the Claw's fault. Jason Kidd got traded a few seasons ago and mine's way too small now anyway.

To be honest, I don't even like watching the actual games anymore. I guess I sort of lost interest. I used to have all the players memorized, but now I can't keep them straight. And nothing even happens until the fourth quarter. I usually spend most of the time spacing out, thinking about school or what's on TV afterwards. But I'd never tell my dad that. It might hurt his feelings. Besides, I sort of like the together time—even if basketball's totally boring.

"Well, Mol," my dad says, interrupting my thoughts as he settles down next to me on the couch. "Big game tonight. Think our boys can handle the Celtics?"

"Definitely," I say, even though I have absolutely no clue. I was sort of hoping the Nets were playing the Hornets. Their cheerleaders, the Honeybees, always wear these really cute outfits covered with tiny bumblebees and honeycombs.

"That's the spirit," my dad says, smiling at me. "Talk about a loyal fan."

It's not true, but I smile back at him anyway. I really want to say something else—some supersmart comment about one of the players or the Nets' chances for the playoffs—but my mind's a total blank. I can't think of a thing. I lean back against the cushions and glance at the TV. The game hasn't started yet and some announcer guy's on-screen, interviewing one of the coaches. I try to focus on what they're saying, but it's sort of hard. I can't stop thinking about the Sophie situation. When I told Tanna about it after school, she said the whole thing would blow over by tomorrow. Julie thought so, too, but I kind of doubt it.

And then there's the Who-Meter. No way is that blowing over any time soon. Tanna won't let it.

Stupid Glenn Borack.

"Hiya, sports fans!" the Claw calls out as she barges into the room. She's carrying a big tray loaded with vegetables.

Squash. Zucchini. Carrots. Everything's cut into thin strips with these weird, ripply edges. And it's all raw.

"Well, well," my dad says, rushing over to help her. He grabs the plate and stares down at it with this big dopey grin on his face. "What have we here?"

"I thought you might like some munchies," the Claw explains, turning toward me. "It's called *cru-di-tés*, Molly. It's French."

My father whistles, like he's never seen asparagus before. "Well it looks just beautiful, Phyllis. Thank you."

I watch as the Claw gives his arm a light squeeze. I feel like giving her arm a squeeze, too. Or even better, a pinch.

"Wasn't that nice of Phyllis?" my dad asks me, after she's gone.

I shrug and shift my eyes back to the screen. The Nets' cheerleaders are warming up on the sidelines. They're wearing these bright-red two-piece outfits that look more like bikinis than uniforms. I don't like them at all. They'll probably fall right off as soon as they jump around.

My dad picks up a piece of celery and dunks it into this weird-looking yellow dip. "Talk about a healthy snack," he says, with a little too much enthusiasm.

"Popcorn's healthy," I point out, not because I'm trying to be difficult, but because it's true. "Corn's a vegetable, too."

"Oh, not like this," he insists. "Popcorn's loaded with oil and salt. This is a lot better." He raises the celery to his mouth and crunches into it. I think I see him wince, but it happens so fast I'm not sure. When he talks again, his voice is soft and a lot more serious. "Come on, Molly. Phyllis put some real effort into this snack." He looks at me. "She's trying to take care of us."

I don't want to be taken care of, I think. Only the thing is: that's not really true. I don't mind if someone takes care of me. I just don't want that someone to be the Claw.

"Here," my dad says, pushing the tray toward me. "Have a carrot."

"I'm not hungry," I mutter.

"Molly—" my dad starts.

"Okay, fine," I say, leaning forward. I grab a carrot and skim it through the disgusting yellow sauce. I shove the whole thing into my mouth and smile superwide. "Yum. Delicious. Best carrot ever."

My dad rolls his eyes. "You're crazy," he says, but his tone is warm. He stretches his arm across the back of the couch

and lets his hand drop onto my shoulder. His eyes hop back to the TV. "Oh, great. Tip-off time. Ready, Mol?"

I pump my head up and down and watch as two players stand next to the ref, their eyes glued to the ball. The ref raises his hands to release it and the players jump, arms outstretched.

"Mitch! Will you come here for a second?" the Claw calls.

My dad leans forward, his eyes still trained on the screen.

"Mitch!" the Claw yells again, louder. "I need you!"

"Be right there!" My dad answers. He gives his head a little shake and pulls himself up off the couch.

"You can't leave," I tell him. "It's bad luck."

"I'll be back in a second," he says. "It'll be like I never left."

"It doesn't matter," I complain. "You're still breaking the rule."

"Oh, I think it'll be okay," my dad says, smiling easily. "You can fill me in on what I miss."

"Whatever," I mutter, slumping lower into the couch. It was stupid to think we'd get to watch the game together anyway. Not with the Claw around, Mitching my dad every chance she gets. And it's only going to get worse. Once they're married I'll bet she makes us throw out the TV altogether.

I grab the remote and switch channels. If my dad doesn't care about the stupid game, why should I? I flip around a little before settling on an old Julia Roberts movie I've never seen before. Something about a girl who keeps getting engaged but then freaks out right before every wedding and runs away.

And that's when it hits me. If Julia Roberts can call off a wedding, why can't my dad? Just because the Who-Meter says it's happening, that doesn't mean it *has* to. Things change.

I call Tanna immediately. "Maybe it's not a totally set thing," I say as soon as she picks up.

"What's not a totally set thing?" she asks.

"The Claw and my dad," I explain. The words come out in a rush. "The wedding. Just because the Who-Meter said so, that doesn't mean—"

"Wait a minute," Tanna says, cutting me off. "I'm on the other line. Hang on."

"Who was that?" I ask when she clicks back.

"Huh? Oh, that was just Gus," Tanna says, like it's no big deal.

I swallow. "What did he want?" I ask. But I already know this wasn't a homework call. The only class Tanna and Gus have together is lunch, which doesn't even count as a real class.

"Nothing," Tanna tells me. "He just wanted to chat. I wasn't really into it, though."

My stomach curls. A boy is calling Tanna? When did this start? And did she just use the word *chat*?

"Does he call a lot?" I try to copy Tanna's breezy, I-so-don't-care voice, but it's hard.

"Not so much," she says. Then adds, "Maybe three or four times before."

I practically drop the receiver. This happened more than once? I wrap the phone cord around my wrist, criss-crossing the line like a bracelet. "Why didn't you ever tell me?"

"Honestly, Molly, it's really not a big deal," Tanna says briskly. "It's actually sort of a waste of time. I mean, Gus is a nice bloke and all—"

"Bloke?" I say, cutting her off.

"Fine, *guy*," Tanna says, huffing into the phone. "He's a nice guy. But it's not like we're going to get *married* or anything."

She's right, I guess. But I still feel weird.

"So what were you saying before," she reminds me. "About the Claw and the Who-Meter?"

I tell Tanna about the Julia Roberts movie and how she ran away from all those fiancés.

"I think I saw that," she says. "It wasn't very good."

"That's not the point," I explain. "The thing is, people call off weddings all the time. Remember that runaway bride from the news? It can happen. Not just in movies but in real life."

"But what about the Who-Meter?" Tanna sounds sort of mad. "Don't you believe the reading?"

"I do. It's not that. It's just—" I take a deep breath and try again. "I think we can *change* the reading."

"I don't know," Tanna says, after a few seconds. "You can't just stop things from happening, Molly."

"I'm not talking about stopping things completely," I push. "But there has to be something we can do."

"I thought you didn't even want to use the machine," Tanna points out. "You wanted to forget about it."

"I did. But this is for a good cause, so it's okay."

"So what. Is that a new rule or something?" Tanna says. "When did you decide?"

"Just now," I admit. I tilt my head back and close my eyes. "He can't marry her. He just can't."

There's a pause on the other end of the line. When Tanna speaks again her voice is clipped. All business. "Fine," she says. "We'll make it happen."

I swallow. "Really? You'll help me?"

"Don't be a ninny. Of course I'll help you," Tanna says, like it's the most obvious thing in the world. "You're my best friend. We'll start planning tomorrow, right after school."

"Thanks," I say, smiling into the phone. I'm so grateful I don't even mind that she just used the word *ninny*.

"Don't worry," she says, as we hang up. "The Claw's going down."

Chapter 8

I HATE THAT we have Social Studies after lunch. The boys are always really sweaty from recess, but Mr. Richards refuses to open the windows because he says the noise from outside distracts us. Sometimes the room smells so bad, I have to breathe through my mouth the whole class, which gives me kind of a headache. Personally, I think a bunch of stinky boys is way more distracting than a few chirping birds, but I guess Mr. Richards doesn't agree.

I open my red spiral notebook and flip to a fresh page. I print the date in the top left corner and then, because I'm nervous and want to look busy, write my name in big block letters.

I really wish Sophie and Tessa weren't in this class. The iPhone thing *just* happened and she's probably still mad.

Gus slides into the seat directly in front of me and turns around. "Hey," he says.

"Hey," I say back, surprised. Gus hardly ever talks to me. Before I can stop myself, I think about Gus calling Tanna. What do they say? What do boys even talk about on the phone? I wonder if he's got her number on speed dial.

"So how come you and Tanna sat alone yesterday?" he asks.

What am I supposed to say? *Well, see, we found this machine that tells you who you're going to marry. Tanna's really excited about it but me, well, I would've been happier with a Sno-Kone maker . . .*

I shrug. "We just felt like it."

If possible, Gus's eyelids droop even lower. "Cool."

He turns back around and, out of the corner of my eye, I see Sophie Kravitz watching us. She punches something into her iPhone and passes it to Tessa, who looks over at me and

giggles. *Why can't she just pass notes like a normal person?* I wonder. Not that that would make me feel any better.

Mr. Richards walks into class and writes a big check mark on the board, which is supposed to remind us all that we're studying our government's system of checks and balances.

I really hope Sophie doesn't think I have a crush on Gus. One: because I don't. And two: because that'll just give her one more reason to hate me. Besides, I'm pretty sure that Gus likes Tanna. Either way, I'm definitely not getting invited to Sophie's next pool party.

I really wish Mr. Richards would crack open a window. I feel like I might throw up. He's talking now, but I can't focus. How can I possibly care about the government being balanced when things in my own life are so completely screwed up?

I try to relax into my chair, but it doesn't work. My legs feel bunched up and my shoulders are tight. I'm mad. Mad at Gus for talking to me and making things worse. Mad at Sophie for being Sophie. I'm even sort of mad at Julie for making me try to throw the basketball, after I told her it wasn't a good idea. But most of all, I'm mad at me. Because when I really think about it, I don't think Sophie is a very nice person. I shouldn't care what she thinks about anything. And I definitely shouldn't want an invite to her stupid party.

But I do. I want her to like me, too. Or at least to stop *not* liking me. Really, is that so much to ask?

Tanna comes home with me after school and the planning officially begins.

"Are you ready for Operation Claw?" she asks, as we walk up the driveway. She's sort of whispering, even though nobody's around.

I nod, as a thrill zings down my spine. "Let's call it OC for short, okay?"

"Smart," Tanna nods. She pats her bag and smiles importantly. "I've got a lot of ideas."

We head inside. The Claw and my dad are standing in the kitchen, drinking coffee.

"What's going on?" I gasp. I look at my dad. "Did you get fired?"

Tanna pokes me in the ribs. "I'll bet she's preggers," she whispers.

I poke her back. Hard.

"Well, it's a pleasure to see you, too," my father says, chuckling. He straightens his bright orange tie. The color reminds me of those Push-Up Pops I used to eat at day camp. "Phyllis wanted me to meet with some wedding photographers this afternoon. I'm heading back to the office now."

"Oh." I try to remember the last time he was home for me after school but can't.

The Claw steps forward. "Well, girls," she announces proudly. "The wedding plans have just entered phase two."

Tanna shoots me a look and I know immediately what she's thinking: *How many phases are there?*

I shrug. *Hopefully four million,* I shoot back.

"Do you know what that means?" the Claw chirps. Her smile's so wide, her teeth look like piano keys.

I shake my head.

The Claw reaches behind the counter and pulls out a Bloomingdale's bag. "Dress time!" She opens the bag and pulls out a long, bright-green velvet dress. Dark green pompoms hang from the hem and neck.

Tanna slaps a hand over her mouth, stifling a gasp.

"You bought me a dress," I say. I can't believe it. I mean, I hate to shop, but I hate looking like a freak even more. And really nothing could possibly be more freakish than the bright-green pom-pom dress. It looks like something straight out of Santa's workshop. Definitely elf material.

"As soon as I saw it, I knew Molly had to have it," the Claw explains to my father. She sounds really proud, like she just invented the Pop-Tart or something. "It's just adorable. The perfect dress for our wedding."

I stare at the Claw. Does she really think the pom-pom dress is cute or is she just trying to torture me? Either way, I'm in big trouble.

Uh-oh. Does this mean she's gonna start shopping for all of my clothes? As if cooking disgusting food and dressing my dad like Baskin-Robbins' sherbet aren't enough. Once my dad and the Claw get married, it's all over. *If they get married,* I remind myself, thinking about OC. It's my only hope.

I wait for my dad to intervene. To protest. To yell. To do something.

Instead, he places his coffee mug in the sink and lifts his briefcase. "Okay, it's back to the salt mines for me," he jokes.

As he leans over to kiss the Claw, my chest pangs and I drop my eyes to the floor.

"Thanks for the help today, Mitch," the Claw croons. "And don't be late tonight, okay? We have that Asian-fusion cooking class."

My dad smooths his tie again and smiles. "Can't wait," he says as he grabs his briefcase from the counter. "Enjoy the dress, Molly."

The sound of the garage door opening makes me want to cry.

"So, what do you say we try it on?" the Claw asks, waving the elf dress in front of my face.

I swallow. "Now?"

The Claw laughs. "Of course now! If it doesn't fit, I might have to take it back."

"It doesn't fit," Tanna says quickly.

"Come on, Molly," the Claw insists, ignoring Tanna. The laughter is gone from her voice. "Right now."

The sooner I try it on, the sooner I can take it off, I think.

I reach out to grab the dress.

"Wait!" Tanna says, lifting her hand. She turns to the Claw. "I'm really sorry, but do you think this can wait until later?

Maybe after dinner?" She clears her throat. "It's just, Molly and I are on sort of a tight deadline."

The Claw wrinkles her brow. "Deadline?"

"Yeah. We're working on a big project down in the basement and wanted to finish it this afternoon." She pauses then adds a very sincere-sounding: "We really love that craft table you set up."

I chew my lower lip. No way is the Claw going to buy this. She's just going to get mad and make me wear an even more hideous dress, if such a thing exists.

"Fine," the Claw says, checking her watch. "I've got to call the caterer anyway." She raises her eyebrows at me as if to say, *You might be off the hook for now, but I'll get you, my pretty.*

As we walk down to the basement, I can almost hear the wicked cackle ringing in my ears.

"Thanks," I tell Tanna once we're safely downstairs. "But what if she asks to see our big project?"

Tanna waves her hand through the air, dismissing my worry. "She won't, believe me. She's in serious Bridezilla mode. If it doesn't have to do with the wedding, she'll forget

all about it." She smiles as she unzips her bag and pulls out her laptop. "Besides, once OC kicks in, she's out of here."

"Why'd you bring that?" I ask, pointing at the computer. Tanna's mom doesn't usually let her bring it to school, since she's worried it'll get broken.

"I told my mom I needed it for a special project," she explains, as her hands move over the keyboard. She's been painting her fingernails dark purple lately and the color always makes me want a grape Jolly Rancher. "We have to write a dating profile."

I look at her. "A what?"

"A dating profile," Tanna explains. "For your dad."

"Wait, *what*?"

Tanna turns the computer toward me and smiles. I glance down at the screen, at a website called NJ-Dates. There's a picture of a couple standing in front of a waterfall, holding hands. Above them the words Date Great, In-State! stretch across the screen in this really loopy cursive. Underneath the couple, in smaller script, it reads: "Brad's from Morristown. Tiffany's from West Orange. Different zip codes. One love: each other."

"Isn't that two loves?" I ask. "I mean, if he loves her and she loves him—"

"Whatever," Tanna says, cutting me off. "I looked at a bunch of different sites, but I think this is the best, since it's only for New Jersey residents. You don't want your dad meeting someone from, like, Florida and making you move away." She glances up from the screen. "Besides, this one gives us a free six-week trial, so we don't need a credit card or anything."

"I don't know," I say. My legs feel sort of fidgety. "I mean, we can't just sign him up."

"Why not?" Tanna demands, like it's no big deal—which for her, it isn't, since we're talking about *my* dad. "Really, Molly, don't be such a boob."

"A *what*?"

"It's the only way," Tanna continues, ignoring me. "If you want him to break up with the Claw, he's got to meet someone else."

I guess she has a point, but the thought of posting my dad up there, right next to Tiffany and Brad, feels sort of wrong. "Maybe we could just try to get him to meet someone from the neighborhood or something?"

"Forget it," Tanna says, matter-of-factly. "If there was anyone around here, he'd have met her already. Besides, this is the way you meet someone if you're not in school."

I stare at the screen. Tiffany and Brad do seem really happy together. And she looks a whole lot nicer than the Claw. I think about the elf dress and my dad's sorbet-colored wardrobe. I swallow. "Fine. But his profile has to be really good."

"Of course," Tanna nods, clicking on to a new page. "We don't want him to meet another Claw."

I shudder.

"Okay, all we have to do is answer a few questions and then NJ-Dates does the rest," Tanna explains.

I lean over her shoulder as we type in my dad's age, occupation, and birthday.

"What are his hobbies?" Tanna asks.

I think back to my dad's life, pre-Claw. There were no Asian-fusion cooking classes, that's for sure. And he definitely watched more TV. CNN and the Nets, plus *American Idol*, which we'd also watch together—except we never rooted for the same contestant. It was more fun that way. And at night my dad tucked me into bed and read *Charlotte's Web*.

A different chapter every night. We read it so many times, we sort of skipped around, depending on our mood.

I actually like pre-Claw dad, but something tells me "*Charlotte's Web* reader" isn't the sort of thing that gets a guy a hot date. Or any date at all.

"How about reading and watching TV," I suggest.

Tanna wrinkles her nose. "That's really boring. Rollerblading in the park's better."

I shake my head. "What park? Besides, my dad doesn't even own Rollerblades."

"Well we can't just put down reading and TV," she insists. "Nobody wants to date someone that lame."

"Hey!" I say, hurt. "My dad's not lame. Besides, it's the truth."

"Oh, relax," Tanna tells me. "I'm not saying your dad's boring. Or that we have to lie. Let's just tweak the truth a little bit. So it sounds more exciting."

I chew my lower lip, thinking. "How about basketball, current events, and spending time with my twelve-year-old daughter?" Tanna's eyebrows arch and I add, "We have to mention me. He can't date someone who doesn't like kids."

"Good point. But let's call you a 'mature twelve-year-old,' so she doesn't think she's getting stuck with a baby." She types then glances at the screen. "Okay, favorite food."

I smile. That one's easy. "Chinese."

"Favorite drink?"

"Definitely coffee. He drinks, like, three cups a day."

Tanna stares at me like I'm insane. "Coffee's way too obvious, Molly. It has to be something really original . . . like . . ." Her face brightens. "A fuzzy navel!"

"Ew!" I shoot back. "That's disgusting."

Tanna rolls her eyes as she types. "It's a drink. You know, a cocktail. It's got peach liqueur in it."

I shrug. It doesn't sound like anything my dad would ever order, but I don't feel like fighting. "Fine. Whatever."

"Okay, we're all done," Tanna announces, after we've answered a few more questions. She hits ENTER and closes the laptop.

"That's it?"

"Yep," she assures me. "Now all we have to do is wait for someone amazing to email your dad. Then you can answer her back and set up a date."

"He's not gonna want to go on a date," I warn. "He's engaged."

"Well, obviously you won't *tell* him it's a date," Tanna explains. "Just make up an excuse to get him to the restaurant or movie theater or whatever." She wrinkles her nose thoughtfully. "Don't forget to pretend you're your dad when you check the account. No adult's gonna make a date with a kid."

"He's gonna be *so* mad."

"Maybe at first," Tanna says, waving her hand dismissively. "But then he'll fall madly in love and it'll all be fine. He'll probably thank you."

I really can't imagine that thank-you, so I don't say anything.

Tanna leans forward, excited. "Hey, let's check the Who-Meter to see if anything's changed."

I look at her. "Isn't it a little early for that? I mean, my dad's profile isn't even up yet."

Tanna shrugs. "Maybe. But it can't hurt. It'll be an experiment. Every time we do something for OC, we'll do another reading."

We take down the Who-Meter and plug it into the wall.

A nervous gurgle bubbles up in my throat as I lean over and twist the dial.

Don't get your hopes up, I tell myself. *It's still way too early for anything to happen.* The wedding bells trip across the screen. And then the basement door slams. I freeze. *The Claw.* Why didn't we lock the stupid door? *Is* there a lock on the stupid door?

"Tanna! Mom sent me over to get you," Milo shouts as he pounds down the stairs. "She says you have to come home right now 'cause you didn't make your bed this morning. You're in big trouble." He leaps from the second to last step, landing on the basement floor.

Tanna and I exchange a look then rush forward. If we can just distract him, maybe he won't see the Who-Meter.

"Whoa! What's that? Can I play?"

Too late. Milo lifts his hand and points at, of course, the Who-Meter.

Chapter 9

THE THING ABOUT Milo is, you just can't get rid of him. He's like Super Glue. If he wants to, he'll hang on forever.

Personally, I don't know why anyone would want to hang out with people who so obviously don't want them around. As much as I'd like Sophie to stop hating me, I'd never follow her like that. It's way too humiliating. Plus, it just wouldn't work. You can't stalk people into liking you.

But that's Milo for you. He really is a major pain. For instance, right now he won't take his grimy eight-year-old hands off of the Who-Meter.

"It sure is ugly," he says, as he flips the dial.

"It's not ugly," I tell him. "It's *antique*. So hands off."

"It's old," he says, sounding totally unimpressed. Still, he keeps pressing all the buttons and tapping the screen which, I notice, stays black. Totally black.

I'm the only one who can work the Who-Meter, I think. I have no idea why, but the machine chose me. It must think I'm special.

My mouth feels all twitchy and I bite my lip to keep from smiling. I don't think it works though, since Tanna says, "What's so funny?"

I shrug and chew a little harder.

"How do you play?" Milo asks.

"Don't touch it," Tanna warns. "It's not a game. It's a, um . . ."

"It's a pizza oven," I rush in, trying to help.

Tanna throws up her hands and tosses me a look like, *You've got to be kidding.*

"A pizza oven?" Milo says slowly. "But where does the dough go?"

Good question. I study the machine. There's really no way the Who-Meter could ever pass as a pizza oven.

"Okay," I say. "It's not actually a pizza oven. It's an old-fashioned television."

"But it doesn't work," Tanna explains. "And Molly and I are trying to fix it."

Milo purses his lips together and tilts his head to one side. I cross my fingers behind my back, hoping he'll drop it.

"But it was just on," he says, pointing at the monitor. "I saw it."

"It comes and goes," Tanna says lightly.

Milo turns to me. "What were you doing to the screen?"

I sigh. Tricking Milo was a whole lot easier when he was four. "I was trying to change the channel," I explain. "But it doesn't get very good reception."

Milo folds his arms across his chest. "You're lying," he announces, very matter-of-factly. He turns to Tanna. "I'm telling."

Tanna chews on her lower lip and I can tell she's trying to decide what to do. I shrug my shoulders as if to say, "Go ahead. You know he means it."

"Fine," Tanna says. "But you have to promise to keep your mouth shut."

Milo grins. "I promise."

"I'm serious. You have to swear."

He pumps his head up and down. "I do, I swear."

"And if you tell, you have to give me all of your Calvin and Hobbes."

"Hey!" Milo looks stricken. He's got this *thing* for Calvin and Hobbes.

"That's the deal," Tanna says. "Take it or leave it."

"Oh, okay," Milo says grudgingly. He points at the Who-Meter. "Now tell me."

So we level with him. Well, almost. We leave out the part about our readings and OC since, really, there's no need to go there. The weird thing is, Milo's not at all impressed. I keep waiting for him to freak out or get really excited or accuse us of trying to trick him again, but he doesn't do any of those things. He basically has no reaction at all. When we turn the machine on and match up his parents, just to show him it works, his eyes widen slightly, but that's it. He doesn't even say, "No way."

In fact, he's totally calm and silent until Tanna says, "You know if you want, Molly can enter your name."

That's when the freak-out happens.

"Ew!" Milo shouts. He backs away from the machine like it's on fire. "Gross! Don't do it!"

"Shhh," Tanna says. "Relax, okay? It's not such a big deal."

"It is," Milo insists. His face is completely white. "It's disgusting."

"You eat your own boogers, but you think the Who-Meter's disgusting?" Tanna shakes her head. "Just don't tell anyone, okay? You promised."

Milo straightens. "I know," he says solemnly. "I won't tell anyone about the Ew-Meter."

"Who-Meter," Tanna and I say, correcting him in unison.

"Well, I call it the Ew-Meter," Milo says, but he's talking so fast it sounds more like *Ewmitter*.

"Oh, sod off," Tanna grumbles.

Milo smiles and I can tell he's really proud of himself.

"I have to go before my mom calls," Tanna tells me. She waves her hand toward Milo. "I'm really sorry about this. I'll see you tomorrow, okay? We can come back here after school."

"I want to come, too," he says in his whiny, Milo-y voice.

Tanna narrows her eyes. "No way. That wasn't a part of the deal and you know it."

"I don't care," he sings, shoving his lower lip out like a bulldog. "If you don't let me play with the Ewmitter, I'll tell."

"But you don't even want to use it," I say, totally exasperated. "You said it was disgusting."

Milo shrugs. "I like your basement."

Little kids make absolutely no sense whatsoever.

"Fine," Tanna says impatiently. "You can hang out with us after school. But you'd better stay out of the way."

"And you'd better keep your mouth shut, too," I say.

"I will, I will," Milo says. He actually sounds annoyed, which is *really* annoying. "I promised, didn't I?"

"Great," I mutter, as we head upstairs. "That makes me feel so much better."

Chapter 10

In social studies the next day, Mr. Richards calls on me to fill in the checks-and-balances triangle he's drawn on the board. As I make my way to the front of the class, Sophie starts to smirk. Out of the corner of my eye, I see her tap something into her iPhone and pass it to Tessa. They both giggle.

I suddenly regret wearing my light-blue cargo pants today, even if they are my favorite. I've worn them a million times and the cloth is so soft, it's almost fuzzy. Still, Tanna says the whole army thing is so fifth-grade and it's time to give the pants a rest.

Mr. Richards holds up his hand, signaling me to stop.

"Sophie and Tessa, would you care to share your joke with the rest of the class?"

The girls straighten in their chairs and shake their heads.

Mr. Richards glances down at Sophie's phone. "You know better than to bring that into my classroom," he says. "Bring it up here, please."

Sophie walks past me and places her phone on his desk, face up. From where I stand, I have a perfect view of the screen.

Don't look down. Don't look down. Don't look down.

But, of course, I look down.

mp is flatr than the brd

Wait, what does that even mean? I wonder. I pick up the chalk and face the triangle.

Forget it. It's not important. It's probably not even about me. But I can't forget. And as I write *Judicial* on the bottom left corner, the stupid line keeps blipping through my head.

mp is flatr than the brd. mp is flatr than the brd.
mp is flatr than the brd.

And then it clicks. My hand freezes. MP is Molly Paige. Molly Paige is flatter than the board.

I'm flatter than the board.

I barely make it through the legislative and executive corners without hyperventilating. The rest of the morning passes in a mortified fog. I keep catching myself staring down at my chest. Sophie Kravitz is right. I really am flatter than a board.

Is it weird that I've never noticed this before? Is this the sort of stuff I should be thinking about, along with wearing cuter clothes and calling boys? Maybe I should make a list.

Here's the thing though: I don't really care about any of that stuff. I don't even mind my flatter-than-the-board chest. Not that I don't *ever* want boobs. But the whole thing just seems like sort of a hassle. The Claw has a ton of bras, which she leaves hanging all over the laundry room. She says they're delicate and can't go into the dryer, but they don't look very delicate to me. They actually look a little like pot holders. They're this really ugly tan color and the straps are like those thick rubber bands. Tanna calls them "gladiator bras" and is always threatening to steal one so Milo can use it as a slingshot.

I know not all bras are like that. The last time Tanna dragged me into American Eagle, I noticed that some of their bras were actually sort of pretty. They come in all different colors and patterns, with matching panties, too. If I were to buy a bra, I think I'd buy one of those.

I definitely don't want one, though.

This past summer Tanna started wearing a bra even though she really doesn't need to. She's almost as flat as I am. Still, she says she likes the support (whatever that means) and that I should respect her right to wear one since she respects my decision not to. And that's fine with me, so long as we don't have to actually talk about it. Just thinking about bras makes my stomach do that weird accordion thing again.

Why did I have to see the stupid note? Now Sophie and Tessa will tell Anne and it'll be their new snotty threesome joke. *Perfect.* And why do they even care about my boobless state anyway? Maybe they're not as flat as I am, but it's not like they have giant coconut boobs either. If you ask me, their chests look more like raisins. Okay, grapes.

At lunch, I have barely any appetite at all.

"What's with you?" Tanna asks. We've switched back to Gus's table, which has me feeling half relieved and half stressed. I want everything to shift back to the way it was, pre–Who-Meter. But I keep sliding my gaze between Gus and Tanna, wondering if they're sending secret "I'll-call-you-tonight" messages between sips of Snapple.

I shrug. "My stomach feels a little funny," I tell her, which isn't exactly a lie.

I still haven't told Tanna about Sophie's note. I almost did, right after it happened, but then something held me back. I guess I feel like lately, the space between us is sort of shifting, growing wider and moving us farther apart. And maybe I can't stop it from happening, but I don't want to help it along either.

"You could get a ginger ale. That might help your stomach," Tanna suggests as she leans forward, lowering her voice. "Any news about OC?"

I shake my head. "I checked the account last night. Only one person answered so far and she wasn't right."

Tanna shoots me a look. "Don't be too picky, Molly," she warns.

"I'm not," I say, thinking about Sheila, who sent a photo of her cat dressed like Santa instead of a picture of herself. She also mentioned that she works in a doughnut shop and admitted to "eating a lot more than I sell." I shake my head again. "This one definitely wouldn't have worked."

"Just remember, the clock's ticking. It's practically February," Tanna says as she spreads ketchup over her hamburger. "Engagements don't last forever."

"Since when do you eat meat?" I ask, pointing at her plate.

Tanna shrugs. "I'm more of a flexitarian now."

"A *what*?"

"A flexitarian," Tanna explains patiently. "We eat meat occasionally." She drops the bun back on the burger and gives it a little pat. "I've been doing some research and just don't think the whole veggie thing will work in England. I mean, they actually eat *kidneys* over there." Tanna makes a face. "So I've decided to adjust my diet accordingly."

"Don't you think you're taking the whole Sir Edmund thing a little too seriously?" I ask.

"Of course I'm taking it seriously," Tanna says, flipping her hair back indignantly. "Molly, this is *marriage* we're talking about."

I can't stop my eyes from sweeping across the room, where Glenn Borack is sitting with a bunch of fifth-grade boys. Two straws dangle from his nostrils as he holds his hands behind his back and bobs his head over a carton of milk.

How am I supposed to take *that* seriously?

When Glenn looks up, I stick my tongue out, quickly, so Tanna won't see and tell me how immature I am. I know it's immature. And I know it's rude, too. But if I can change my dad's reading, maybe I can change my own. No way will Glenn Borack want to marry me if he thinks I'm a meany.

Glenn's eyes widen with surprise. Then he shoots his tongue out of his mouth and waggles it around, in between the two straws. He looks like he's trying to catch flies or something.

Gross.

On the other hand, our unmarriage is off to a pretty good start.

I empty my tray and head out to the playground to meet Julie.

"Ready to shoot some hoops?" she asks, tossing me the basketball. I manage to graze it with my left hand before missing completely.

I chase down the ball and, on my way back, notice for the first time that Julie has boobs. Serious boobs. Not quite grapefruits but definitely in the citrus family. How could I not have noticed them before? In science, Mrs. Craven told us that almost fifty percent of men are color-blind. Is there such a thing as being boob-blind?

"If you don't feel ready, we can totally stick to dribbling," Julie assures me, misinterpreting the horrified look on my face. "I just thought you might want to try something new."

"No, it's okay . . . but listen, do you wear a bra?" *Whoa.* Did I really just say that out loud? I watch as the color rushes into Julie's cheeks. "I'm so sorry. I can't believe I—"

"No," Julie interrupts, her cheeks fading slightly. "It's just weird that you mentioned it, that's all. My mom and I got into a huge fight about bras last night."

"That is weird," I admit. I can't even imagine saying the word *bra* in front of my dad. And I'd rather die before talking to the Claw about any of this stuff.

"She says I have to start wearing normal bras instead of just sports bras all the time."

I shake my head. "I don't even know what that is."

Julie looks around, then stretches out the neck of her T-shirt, revealing a thick gray strap of sweatshirt material. "*That's* a sports bra," she explains. "I like them because they don't look all bra-y. Plus, they sort of flatten me out."

"Why doesn't your mom want you to wear them?" I ask. I place the ball on the concrete and sit down on top of it. Julie drops down beside me.

She shrugs. "She says they're really only for sports, and that I should bring one with me to school every day and change for PE." She rolls her eyes. "Can you imagine walking around all day long with a *bra* just sitting at the bottom of your backpack? I mean, what if I'm looking for a pencil and accidentally pull it out?"

We look at each other and start to giggle.

"I can't even imagine owning a bra," I admit.

Julie's smile disappears. "I know. I hate it." She looks down at the ground. "I still can't believe I need one."

I search my brain for something nice to say. "I didn't even notice you did, until this afternoon," I tell her. "Besides, at least you're not flat like me. Sophie Kravitz says I'm flatter than a board."

"Some people," Julie says, running her fingers through her shiny black hair, "are chest obsessed."

I giggle again. "Is that like having boobs on the brain?"

"Or mammary madness?" Julie laughs then quickly explains: "*Mammary* is another word for 'boob.' My mom's a doctor."

"Hey, I like that." I grin. "Sophie Kravitz is mad about mammaries."

We fall back on the pavement, laughing hysterically. My arms and legs relax into the concrete and I prop my head up against the basketball. The sun toasts my face and I feel warm, inside and out.

By the time the bell rings for the end of the day, my head feels lighter and the knots in my stomach have untangled. On the bus, I'm not even that annoyed when Milo and his little friend Josh sit directly in front of Tanna and me.

"Don't forget, I'm coming over to your house," Milo informs me with this ultrabrat smile on his face.

I roll my eyes. "Don't remind us, okay?"

Josh turns around and looks right at me.

"Are you guys going to see the Ewmitter now?" he asks loudly. His eyes are as round as doughnuts. "Can I come?"

I look around to see if anyone heard. Thankfully, our bus driver, Rodney, is blasting Fergie, so it looks like we're safe. But *still.* I turn to Milo, absolutely furious. Tanna punches the back of his seat and he bounces forward, then back.

"Ow!" he yelps. His face is bright red.

"I'm so taking all your Calvin and Hobbes," Tanna informs him.

"No fair! I just told Josh!" he sputters. "That's it, I swear. He won't tell anyone!"

"I won't," Josh promises. "I just want to see it."

Tanna and I exchange a look. The only thing worse than being blackmailed by an eight-year-old is being blackmailed by two eight-year-olds.

The bus lurches to a halt in front of my house.

"Oh, come on," I say, grabbing my backpack.

Inside, we stop by the kitchen to grab some Oreos and read the Claw's note ("Out with the florist, back by six!") then head down to the basement. I plug in the Who-Meter and it starts to hum.

"So," I tell Josh. "Here it is."

"Wow," he breathes. His mouth is so full of cookie that his words sound sort of muffled. "It sure is ugly."

"It's *antique*," I correct. "Ever heard of retro?"

Josh shakes his head, totally unimpressed. "Can we try it out?"

I shrug. "Why not?" I smile, remembering Milo's reaction yesterday. "Want me to put your name in?"

"No way," Josh says firmly, swallowing his last bite of Oreo. "But how 'bout my sister?"

"Your sister?" I ask, surprised. I'm a little disappointed my suggestion didn't trigger a Milo-style freak-out.

Josh nods. "Her name is Ellie and she's really old. She's in college and every time she comes home, she has a new boyfriend."

"And you're telling us this because . . . ?" Tanna asks, flicking a chip of purple polish off her nail.

"If I know the name of the boy she's going to marry, I won't have to bother with any of the others," Josh explains. He wrinkles his nose like he's just smelled something really awful. "The new ones all think they have to play catch with me in the backyard." He shakes his head mournfully. "And I don't even *like* sports."

I look at Tanna.

"Might as well," she says. "He's already seen it."

So I turn to the Who-Meter and find out that Josh's sister is going to marry someone named Nathaniel Jeremy Koslov. And even though Josh has no idea who Nathaniel Jeremy Koslov is, he's thrilled.

"This is gonna save me a lot of time," he says. "Thanks."

Everyone smiles.

"That was sort of cool," Tanna says, after he leaves.

"Definitely," I agree.

Later that night, as I slip into bed, I decide that today turned out surprisingly well. It definitely hit a low point around Social Studies, but then things sort of turned around. And Tanna and I used the Ewmitter for good. Again. We're practically humanitarians.

This must be what Angelina Jolie feels like every day, I think as I drift off to sleep.

When I wake up the next morning, I'm in a great mood. And then I step onto the bus.

"There's been a new development," Tanna informs me as I slide in beside her.

"What are you talking about?" But as I ask the question,

I notice that everyone is staring at me. Not in a mean way or anything. They just look really, really interested.

Max Dreyfuss taps me on the shoulder. For the first time this whole year, he actually speaks in his normal, nonburpy voice. "Can I try the Ewmitter?" he asks.

As the entire bus erupts into a giant chorus of *me-toos* and *how-about-mes* I slide down in my seat and squeeze my eyes shut.

Before I accept another promise from an eight-year-old, I'm definitely going to define the word *promise* first.

Chapter 11

Everyone's talking about the Ewmitter. This isn't just me being paranoid. *Everyone* really is talking about it. I think I'm cursed. Seriously, how else can you explain it? All that Ouija-fortune-telling-horoscope stuff must have angered a vindictive spirit and this is their revenge. Or maybe it's punishment for my being mean to Gross Glenn which—if that's the case—really isn't fair, since he was mean right back.

"What are we gonna do?" I ask Tanna. We're standing in front of her locker and I swear even Nick Jonas is looking at me differently. "What if somebody tells their parents?"

Tanna pats my shoulder. "Oh, don't get your knickers in a twist," she says calmly. "Personally, I think Milo and Josh did us a favor."

I stare at her. "Are you crazy? And why are you talking like that? What are knickers?"

"Even if someone does tell, no parent would ever believe them," she reasons, ignoring my questions.

I can't believe it. Tanna's actually *happy* about this! And what's with the weird accent? It's been fading in and out all morning, but she definitely sounds strange. Strangely *British.*

"The way I see it," she continues as she pulls a few books out of her locker and slams the door shut, "is, everyone knowing is a *good* thing."

"Did you hit your head last night? I mean, have you completely lost your . . ." I trail off as I look down, past her lavender blouse to her bright purple pants. They're short and button just below the knees. "What are those?"

"They're new," she says quickly. "Look, don't be so negative. There's nothing wrong with letting people use the machine . . . for a modest fee, of course."

"You want to *charge* people to use the Ewmitter?" I ask, but of course I already know the answer.

Tanna straightens slightly as Gus rounds the corner, his backpack slung over his shoulder. He stops in front of us.

Please don't ask about the Ewmitter, I beg silently. *Please don't ask about the Ewmitter.*

"Hey," he says to Tanna.

"Hi," Tanna says, flipping her hair. She waves her hand in my direction. "We're, um, sort of in the middle of something here."

Gus dips his head slightly and I find myself actually feeling sorry for him.

"No problem," he says. "I'll, uh, see you at lunch?"

Tanna shrugs. "I guess so."

Gus hesitates slightly, then says "See ya" and shuffles down the hall. As I watch him go, I notice that his shoulders look a little more hunched than usual.

I turn to Tanna. "Don't you think you were a little harsh?" I ask. "I thought you liked Gus."

She sighs. "I think I have to tell him."

"If he doesn't know about the Ewmitter yet, he will. It's all over school."

"No, not about that. About me. And Sir Edmund." Tanna

smooths the ruffles on her blouse and tugs at her weird half-pants. "It might help him understand."

I blink. "Understand what?"

She looks at me like I might just be the densest person in the world. "Why we shouldn't talk anymore," she explains. "It's just a waste of time. I mean, say we do go out. So what?"

I watch as her face twists into a sort of torn expression and her chin juts forward, the way it does when she's frustrated. *She likes Gus,* I think. *She* really *likes Gus.* The thought of my best friend having an actual boyfriend makes my stomach twist around until it's kind of hard to breathe. I just don't get it. On the other hand, shutting down your whole life because of the Ewmitter doesn't make a whole lot of sense either.

"But what if the reading changes?" I ask. "Think about my dad and the Claw."

"Different," Tanna says, slamming her locker door shut. "Totally different."

"Why?"

Tanna clicks her tongue in a *You're-hopeless!* sort of way. "Because we're purposely trying to break them up," she ex-

plains. "It's like, an experiment. Nobody's doing that with Sir Edmund and me."

"Okay, fine. You and this Sir Edmund guy are going to be a couple," I say, trying again. "But who knows when? And if you and Gus have fun together, what's the big deal?"

Wait, did I just offer relationship advice? That's so *not* my department.

Tanna looks at me the way we both look at Milo.

Oh, grow up. That's what she's thinking. I just know it.

"You're right," she says. "It *wouldn't* be a big deal. Because of Edmund, nothing will. So why bother?"

"I don't know," I say, honestly. It's not like I'm a couples' therapist or anything. Besides, if you ask me, all boys are a total waste of time. But because I don't want to suffer through another look I keep my mouth shut.

"Oh, forget it," Tanna says. "I won't tell him. It'll just make things weird. Besides, he'll understand when it's his turn."

My stomach skids. "His turn for what?"

"To use the Who-Meter," Tanna explains, like it's the most obvious thing in the world. "I'm thinking we charge five dollars."

"No way," I tell her.

"Fine. Six then."

"It's not the money," I say. "I can't have the entire school sneaking around my basement."

Tanna laughs. "Duh! They won't! Well, not all at once. We have to be organized about it. We can see a few clients each day. You know, after school."

"Clients?"

"I just wish people would stop calling it the Ewmitter," she gripes, rushing on. "I mean, it just sounds so *bleh*. . . . What do you think of the Wow-Meter instead?"

I shake my head. I really don't know what to say. Plus, Tanna's faux English accent is back and it's sort of hard to understand her.

"And we have to do something about the presentation."

"The presentation?" I repeat. I can feel my forehead wrinkling.

"Definitely," she says, screwing up her nose in distaste. "It's just so old and dusty. Maybe we could paint it? I'm thinking violet." She turns to me. "Or is that too girly?"

I grip my backpack. "Cut it out, okay? You know we can't do this."

"You're so negative, Molly," Tanna says, but her voice is

soft and I can tell she's not really angry. "Remember what you said, about using the Who-Meter for a good cause? Well, this would be *lots* of good causes."

"I don't know," I say, feeling torn—and a little queasy. I think back to yesterday and how great it felt to help Josh. But then I think back even further, to the day we found the machine—and how it matched me with Glenn Borack. *That* didn't feel great. Not at all. On the other hand, if I can un-Mitchify my dad *and* convince Glenn Borack to hate me, the Who-Meter will have totally saved me. Twice. Maybe lots of other kids need saving, too.

"But what if an adult finds out?" I ask, picturing the Claw. *Yikes. Big yikes.*

Tanna blows air out of her mouth as the first bell rings. "Just think about it, okay? Keep an open mind."

My mind is wide open, I want to say. *The answer is NO.* But when I turn to Tanna, the words freeze in my throat.

"Fine," I hear myself say as we head into homeroom.

All morning long, I feel totally on display. It's like I'm sitting inside a huge glass tank and everyone's watching. I don't think I'll ever be able to visit the aquarium again. It's *that* weird. Kids I don't even know say hi to me in the halls and at least three kids save me a seat in every class. In French, when I forget that *fenêtre* means "window," nobody laughs. Not even Max Dreyfuss.

I know I should be enjoying the attention. But I can't. Because every time I turn around, someone new is watching me, waiting to ask about the Ewmitter. That's all anyone really cares about.

I just keep repeating exactly what I heard Posh and Becks say during this E! interview when the reporter asked them how many kids they were planning to have. "No comment."

By the time recess rolls around, I'm really looking forward to seeing Julie. But when I get out on the playground it occurs to me that that might feel strange, too. Maybe the Ewmitter's changed everything.

"Are you mad I didn't tell you?" I ask.

"No," Julie says. She passes me the basketball. "It's just sort of hard to believe."

"It is," I say, relieved. The ball zooms toward me and, without even thinking, I reach out and grab it. Julie flashes me a congratulatory smile.

"So, this thing you guys found," she says slowly, as if trying to make sense of the situation. "It actually works?"

"I think so," I say. Before I know it, we're passing the ball back and forth and I'm telling her the whole story, starting with the Claw's lame arts-and-crafts center and my Glenn Borack reading (at this point, Julie's eyebrows shoot up and she lets out a panicked, "Oh, no!" before backpedaling with a calmer, "Um, he's not so bad.") right up to Tanna's business scheme this morning.

"Wow," Julie breathes. "So what are you gonna do?"

"Well, obviously I have to tell her to forget it," I say. I catch the ball, wobble a little then toss it back. It sails neatly into Julie's arms. "It's just, Tanna's not so easy to say no to sometimes."

"I can see that," she says, but not in a mean way.

We're silent for a minute, and I listen to the sound of the ball swooshing back and forth between us. Remembering what Tanna said about using the Ewmitter for good, I look up.

"But I do want to use it a little," I admit. "You know, as an experiment."

Julie's forehead puckers. "Experiment?"

"Yeah. To see if I can change my reading." I throw the ball then add, "and my dad's."

"I don't get it," Julie says. She grabs the ball and rests it against her hip.

I shrug. "If I'm a jerk to Glenn, he's not gonna want to marry me. And if I can get my dad to meet someone else, he won't marry the Claw. So I thought I'd just keep checking the machine to see . . ." I trail off and look at Julie. She's just standing there, with this worried look on her face.

"I don't know," she says, after a minute. "It sounds sort of . . . risky."

"Risky how?" I ask, surprised and a little disappointed. "It could totally save me."

"Maybe," Julie says, but I can tell she doesn't really mean it.

"Well, what would you do?"

"What? With the Ewmitter?" She frowns slightly. "Probably nothing."

"At all?" I ask. "You wouldn't even use it for yourself?"

She lifts her arm and throws. "I guess it feels kind of like reading the last page of a mystery before you've even started."

Well, that makes sense. I glance around the playground and spot Glenn Borack playing dodgeball with a group of

fifth-graders. He's got one finger up his nose and is wiggling it around, like it's no big deal. When he catches me looking at him he flashes a big, stupid smile and—finger still inserted in nostril—sticks out his tongue.

In my case, the book would be a tragedy, not a mystery.

"I really hope my plan works," I say. I glare at Glenn and toss the ball, which Julie catches easily.

She follows my gaze. "Maybe you won't need it," she says as she throws. "Glenn might get cute when he's older."

Impossible, I think, but since I know she's just trying to make me feel better, I smile and stretch my arms out wide.

When recess is over, I grab my books and head to Social Studies.

I've decided. I'm going to do it. I'm going to tell Tanna to forget the whole thing. It's way too risky. Sure, on a specific, case-by-case basis the Who-Meter might be a big help. Like when dealing with horrible step-monsters-to-be and nosepicking future husbands. But letting the whole school use it? No way. Not happening. Case closed.

I smile to myself as I walk through the door.

And then I stop.

I shouldn't be surprised. But of course I am. Sophie and Tessa are sitting in the middle of the room, smiling and waving. Correction: Sophie and Tessa are sitting in the middle of the room, smiling and waving at *me*.

Chapter 12

OKAY, SO I lied. The attention feels pretty good. Of course, I know it doesn't mean anything. Sophie and Tessa only saved me a seat because of the Ewmitter. That's why I smiled and waved back at them but then sat at my usual desk, a few chairs over. And when, halfway through class, Sophie flashed me her phone, which read: "Mall after skool?" I told her I was busy.

Still, a part of me was thrilled. Sophie Kravitz wants to be seen in public with *me*. Again, I realize this wasn't a genuine BFF invite. The minute we got to the mall—maybe even on the ride over—she'd start pumping me about the machine.

It was so painfully obvious that the whole idea should have made me mad.

Only it didn't. Instead, I felt relieved. It was a relief to be able to get through class without worrying about being the target of another poisonous iPhone text. It was a relief to know that the Ewmitter had solved the Sophie problem. And, okay, I'll admit it: it was a relief to know that I could—if I wanted—hang out after school with the most popular girl in my grade.

But then I started thinking about the *whole* situation. And that's when I got that carsick feeling again. Because the thing is, it won't last. None of it. If I don't let everyone use the Ewmitter, they'll gradually forget about the machine.

And they'll forget about me right along with it.

All the attention will just go away.

This morning, that's exactly what I wanted. Only now that Sophie's being nice, I'm not so sure I do. Besides, isn't the Sophie situation just one more example of the Ewmitter doing good? Maybe it's selfish of me to hog it all to myself.

On the other hand, how can I start a secret marriage business in my basement? Seriously, who does that? It's not like

selling rhinestone barrettes at lunch or having a paper route after school.

By the time the final bell rings, I'm a total stress mess. When Tanna reminds me that she has a dentist appointment, I'm so relieved I practically faint. If she came over, she'd definitely want to talk about the Ewmitter. And the only thing I'm really in the mood for is a big bag of Doritos. I can practically taste the cheesy goodness.

As soon as I get home, I grab the bag, plop myself in front of the computer and check the NJ-Dates account. My dad's got four new messages: three are duplicates from a woman named Cheryl who's got pink hair and, according to her last email, lots of computer problems. The fourth message is from someone named Daisy Palmer.

To: mitchellp@njdates.com
From: dpalm@njdates.com

Hi, Mitchell:

I've actually never done any online dating before (does everyone start their emails that way?) and to be honest, I wasn't entirely sure I was going to

go through with this until I read your profile. It struck me as very honest and not out to impress (but in a good way!) so I decided to get in touch. Hmm . . . what else to write? I'm almost 40 (should I have lied? Oops!) and manage a Barnes & Noble while I pursue a degree in library sciences. I don't have any kids of my own but am very close with my nieces and nephews (I have six! Claire is Molly's age and she too is very sophisticated ☺). I'm sort of shy and love to read—but I also enjoy going to the movies and the occasional play. If any of the above interests you, please feel free to write back.

Take care

Daisy

P.S. I've never had a fuzzy navel, but I do love peaches!

I open the attached picture. Much to my relief, it's not a cat but an actual person—a woman with curly brown hair and big blue eyes. Her head's sort of lowered, like she's reading something, and her smile's warm and friendly.

She looks nice, I decide. Not like the sort of person who would banish a bunch of kids to a basement or ruin a Nets game with a lot of gross French vegetables.

Daisy Palmer and Mitchell Paige. Daisy, Mitchell, and Molly Paige.

The more I repeat the names, the more I like the way they sound. I hit REPLY and then my fingers freeze over the keyboard.

According to OC, I'm supposed to answer as my dad and I'm supposed to set up a date. But I'm not really sure how to do either of those things. And what if Daisy Palmer isn't as normal as she looks? What if she's a crazed maniac posing as a sweet library sciences student (what *is* that?) in order to capture her next victim?

My poor dad. This is all my fault.

I take it back. It's Tanna's fault, and she should be here, instead of getting her teeth cleaned. She'd know exactly what to do. But she won't be home for another few hours and if I call Julie, she'll probably just tell me to stop meddling and go with the flow. I'm not sure I'm in a flow sort of mood, so I'm totally on my own here.

I'm still trying to decide what to do when the front door slams.

"Molly, are you home?" the Claw calls. "I need to speak with you!"

To be continued, I think, as I put the computer to sleep and follow the Claw's voice into the living room. She's sitting on the couch, sandwiched between the elf dress and a really strange-looking man. He's supershort and his flat brown hair is combed all the way forward, forming a little triangle in the middle of his forehead.

Maybe she's having an affair, I think hopefully.

"Molly, meet Maurice," the Claw says. "Maurice, meet Molly."

Maurice smiles at me, offering his damp hand.

We shake and I resist the urge to wipe my palm off on my pants.

"Maurice is the tailor who will be handling all alterations for the wedding," the Claw says, in the same voice you'd use to introduce the president. "I thought we could start with your dress."

Okay, now I really wish Tanna were here. She got me out of the last fitting. I know she'd be able to get me out of this one, too. Without her, I'm one dead elf.

I drag the dress into the bathroom and hang it on the

back of the door. I swear the stupid pom-poms are laughing at me.

I can tell almost immediately that it doesn't fit. It's way too easy to pull on and whenever I move these weird cloth balloons bubble up under my arms.

"Too loose in the bust," Maurice announces loudly when I walk back into the living room. He jabs my chest with his finger. "We'll have to take it in. You'll have *a lot* of leftover material. You want me to make a wrap?"

"That won't be necessary," the Claw says. She sounds chipper and I wonder if she enjoyed the comment about my chest. She turns to me. "It's perfect, right?"

"It itches," I tell her.

The Claw frowns. "It can't. It's velvet. Velvet doesn't itch."

I frown right back at her. "It feels like it's made of horsehair."

"Molly, this was a very expensive dress and I expect a little cooperation," she says. "I'd hate to have to tell your father about this."

Her smile makes me wonder if she painted her dark red fingernails with real blood. I shoot her my best *I-might-have-to-live-with-you-but-I-don't-have-to-like-you* glare in response.

The Claw sighs. "Maybe it's just stiff," she says. "We'll have it dry-cleaned before you wear it."

Maurice pulls a stiletto-shaped pincushion from his bag. "Don't worry," he tells me. "When I'm through with you, you're gonna look like a young . . . Liza Minelli."

Um, *who*? And why is everyone suddenly talking about my concave chest? That's two times in two days. It can't be that noticeable.

Or is it? Maybe there's something really wrong with me. I glance down at myself. It doesn't look so strange to me, but I guess I'm used to it.

I wonder if my mother was flat, too. Maybe it runs in the family? I close my eyes, trying to remember, but all I can picture is hair. Lots and lots of red hair. Not my way-too-bright orange-red but a cooler, silky auburn that smells like perfume and clean laundry.

I think about my favorite picture of her, which is behind me on the mantel. In it, she's sitting on our old couch, holding a book and smiling at the camera. She looks like the sort of person who could talk to anyone. There's something about that picture that makes me want to crawl inside it and curl up. My dad told me he took it about a year before I was born, but what I've always wondered about is what happened after he put the camera down. Did my mom scoot over on the couch to make room for him? Or did she just pick up her book and start reading again? I've got a million different versions of that day in my head, but I don't know if any of them are right. It was a long time ago and my dad doesn't remember anymore.

My arms and legs relax a little under the stiff fabric. And then Maurice starts poking me with pins.

"Watch it!" I yelp. "I'm not a voodoo doll."

The Claw's lips twitch. I'll bet she bought the dress too big on purpose.

I turn my head toward the fireplace. My eyes skip down the stone mantel, looking for the familiar silver frame.

Only it's gone. There's an empty place where it usually rests, in between a blue vase and my fifth-grade class picture. Tiny prickles run up and down my arms. And they have absolutely nothing to do with Maurice and his bloodthirsty pins.

What happened to my mom's picture?" I ask the Claw and my dad, later that night. We've just sat down to dinner and the Claw is dishing out huge servings of something called turkey marsala.

I close my eyes and try to imagine that it's moo shu chicken from Hunan Park. That's the only way I'll ever be able to swallow a bite.

"What picture is that?" the Claw asks breezily as she passes my dad a plate of gray meat.

"The one that should be on the mantel but isn't," I counter. "I looked everywhere, but it's gone."

The Claw tilts her head to one side thoughtfully. "I'll have to ask Mara about that."

"Cleaning ladies clean things," I point out. "They don't move them."

The Claw's skeleton-thin eyebrows arch so high they practically disappear into her hairline. "Excuse me, Molly, but I don't think I like your tone."

My father clears his throat. "I didn't notice it was gone," he says. "But I'm sure it'll turn up."

He didn't notice. The only picture of my mother we have

out in the entire house and my father doesn't even bother to keep track of it. I try to catch his eye, but he's reading the I Can't Believe It's Not Butter container and doesn't look up.

I stand, my chair scraping against the tile floor. "I think I'll go look some more."

"*Someone*'s wedding jitters came early," the Claw says as I head out the front door. When I look back over my shoulder, my father's bent so low over the I Can't Believe It's Not Butter, he's practically kissing the plastic tub.

It's still light outside and—because I want to keep busy and because it's the only place there is to look in my front yard—I start rooting around the recycling piled at the curb.

It's pretty disgusting. I wonder if this is some sort of health hazard.

Good. I hope I cut my hand on a rusty can and get tetanus. I'll die and my dad will feel awful. In his grief-stricken state he'll blame the Claw and call off the wedding.

She's *so* not invited to the funeral.

Speaking of funerals, I wonder how many people will come to mine. I'll bet Mrs. Sixsmith makes some sort of phony speech about what a good sport I was.

Uh-oh. What if my dad buries me in the elf dress? He's sort of clueless that way.

That's it. I'm definitely haunting him.

"Eye are oo 'igging aroun ih da garbash?"

Startled, I jump to my feet, just in time to see Glenn Borack hop off his bike. Over his winter coat, he's wearing a helmet, elbow and kneepads, and a mouth guard that completely garbles his speech.

Great. I'm really not in the mood to socialize right now. Not like I'm *ever* going to be in the mood to socialize with Gross Glenn. Even if I wanted to, it'd be impossible. I mean, what am I supposed to do? Have a polite talk about the weather when the whole time all I'll really be thinking is: *You're my future hubby. You're my future hubby. You're my future hubby.*

Yuck. Forget it.

"I'm not," I say, glaring at him. "Go away."

Glenn unbuckles his helmet and spits his mouth guard into his hand *(double yuck!)*. "You are, too," he states calmly. His face suddenly brightens. "Hey, did you lose something?"

"Why are you wearing all that stuff?" I ask, trying to change the subject.

"My mom's a little overprotective," he says, like it's no big deal he's practically wrapped in a gymnastics mat. He kneels down beside me. "You know, last year my dad accidentally threw out his wallet. We tore apart the garbage looking for it."

"Did you find it?" I ask, in spite of myself.

"*I* did," Glenn says proudly. "It was in an empty milk carton." He starts sifting through a clear blue bag filled with bottles. "If you tell me what you lost, I'll look, too."

"Forget it," I tell him. "Leave me alone."

Glenn doesn't move. "This is a lot of garbage," He points out. "You'll finish faster if I help."

Wow. Talk about persistent. I wonder if he pesters me into marrying him, too. Maybe that's the only reason we wind up together.

"Fine," I snap. "It's a picture."

Glenn empties the bag onto the sidewalk.

"You don't even know what picture you're looking for," I say, glaring at him.

"How many pictures did your family throw away today?" he counters.

Okay, he's got a point.

I lower my head and try to focus on the pile of newspapers in front of me. *Let's see, there's the* Wall Street Journal, *the* New York Times, *the* Daily Record . . . *Oh, wow. What if I can't change the reading after all? What if I'm stuck with Gross Glenn?* I can't do it. I just can't sit next to Glenn Borack and not wonder about our maybe-marriage. Or what our maybe-wedding will be like. Or how many maybe-kids we'll have.

And what if Glenn asks about the Ewmitter? Almost everyone else at school has. What should I say? He can't know anything about my reading. Not ever. I try to ignore him, but it's sort of hard. My insides feel all jumpy. At least Glenn isn't trying to talk to me. He's just sitting there, calmly sorting and sifting.

He doesn't say a word. Not even when he hands over the silver-framed picture, hops onto his bike, and pedals off.

I shouldn't feel guilty, I tell myself as I head back inside. So what if I didn't thank him? I didn't ask for his help in the first place. Besides, I totally would have found the picture on my own—that pile was next . . .

This is *completely* the Claw's fault.

I pause just outside the den, where my dad's watching the news. I'm tempted to march in with the recovered picture. *How do you like your fiancée now?* I could say, and drop it on his lap.

But instead, I decide to wait. Let him come to me.

Only he never does. At the end of the night, when I'm brushing my teeth, I hear him click off the television and climb the stairs.

"Goodnight, Molly," he whispers from the hall. He walks into his bedroom and closes the door.

The house is so quiet I feel like screaming.

I tiptoe downstairs and turn on the computer. I click open Daisy's email and hit REPLY.

> Dear Daisy:
>
> Thanks for writing! Working at Barnes & Noble sounds very interesting—do you get free books? I'd really like to meet for a movie or a play sometime soon but, unfortunately, I'm going on a business trip tomorrow and will be away for a pretty

long time. Do you mind emailing for a while, then maybe we can meet in person?

Sincerely,

Mitchell Paige

P.S. Thank you for not calling me Mitch. I really hate that.

P.P.S. If you like peaches, you should definitely try Ben and Jerry's Country Peach Cobbler. Molly loves it!

I reread the note once and, before I can change my mind, hit SEND.

Back in my room, I wipe off my mother's picture and place it on the nightstand. As I slip into bed, I think about October and how my dad was right. It really is a lot sooner than I thought.

I stare at the shadows on the ceiling, remembering how they used to scare me. When I woke up in the middle of the night I'd keep my eyes shut until my dad came into the room and turned on the lights. Then we'd go downstairs for hot chocolate. (The real kind, with marshmallows. Not that powdery diet stuff the Claw always buys.)

Tanna's mom won't let her have chocolate at night. She says it hypes you up, but I don't think that's right. I always fell right back to sleep afterwards.

I flip over onto my stomach and bury my face into the pillow. What I need, I decide, is a distraction. Something to take my mind off of the Claw and that stupid elf dress.

Maybe Tanna's Ewmitter scheme isn't all that bad an idea. I mean, the secret's already out and, this way, the machine will be able to help even more people. Plus, it'll definitely keep me busy.

Of course, I'll have to do some major lying when it comes to the Claw.

But I'll just think of that as an added plus.

Chapter 13

THE NEXT MORNING on the bus, I tell Tanna the good news.

"We can open the Ewmitter business, but only if we follow these rules," I say, handing her the list I wrote during breakfast.

"Smashing!" she shouts, waving the slip around. "Simply corking!"

I stare at her. Today's she's wearing a plaid kilt, a grape cardigan, and a violet beret.

"Aren't berets French?" I ask.

"It was the only hat I could find that wasn't a ski mask,"

she reasons. "And English women are big on hats and since France is so close to England—"

I raise my hand. "Forget it. Just try to talk like a normal person, okay?"

"We have so much to do," she says, ignoring me. "Do you think we can open this afternoon?"

"We need to be clear on the rules first," I say.

Tanna rolls her eyes, but she unfolds the piece of notebook paper.

"'Only one kid at a time can be in the basement for a reading,'" she recites, then looks up. "So what, we only see one client a day? That's not very good business sense, Molly."

"No," I say. "We can see more. But everyone else needs to wait in the backyard until it's their turn."

"Why?"

I point back to the list.

"'All results are confidential,'" Tanna reads. "'And no laughing, no matter what.'" She flips her hair back. "Well, duh. Of course. If we're going to do this we have to be mature."

"Right," I say. For obvious Glenn Borack–related reasons, I feel very strongly about the no-laughing rule. "If people want to compare their results or something that's up to them. But *we* have to keep our mouths shut." I pause, letting this last rule sink in. "Okay, read the next one."

"'All Ewmitter users must be sworn to secrecy,'" Tanna recites, lowering her head over the list. "'They can discuss the machine with other Ewmitter-aware friends, but they can't spread the word.'" She looks at me and shrugs. "I'm not so sure we can control that one, but no problem. *Now* are we open for business?"

I shake my head. "We're not done with the rules yet."

"Blimey," Tanna mutters, returning to the sheet. "'Number four: The Claw CANNOT be home for any of this.'" She frowns. "I see your point, but that could be sort of a problem."

"It could be," I say, smiling. "But since I swiped her Blackberry last night, it isn't."

Tanna's face relaxes. "Brilliant. When's our opening?"

"The Claw goes to the gym Monday, Wednesday, and Friday afternoons. Her 'Booty Blast' class lasts an hour."

"Perfect," Tanna says as the bus rolls to a stop in front of school and Rodney cuts the Alicia Keys he's been blasting. "That'll definitely give us enough time to see four or five clients." She puckers her forehead, thinking. "At ten dollars a head, that's not so bad."

I grab my backpack and stand. "Wait, I thought you said six dollars a person?"

"I've re-evaluated," Tanna says briskly. "So, it's Wednesday. Are we ready to book our first clients?"

"I guess so," I say as we move into the aisle.

"I'll handle the schedule," Tanna says.

"Why can't we both do it?"

"It'll get too confusing," she says firmly. "What if we start double-booking? Besides, *you're* the one who can work the machine." There's a sharpness in her voice that catches me off-guard.

"So?"

"So, that's your job," Tanna explains. "And scheduling will be mine. It's an even split."

I'm not so sure she's right—or who has the better job—but I drop it. And that's that. We're officially open for business.

By midmorning, Tanna informs me that the entire month is all booked up and she's started a wait list. At lunch, we're

bombarded with offers of free DVDs, candy, and Abercrombie gift certificates—all from kids who want their appointments to be bumped up.

"New rule," I tell Tanna as Max Dreyfuss passes her a bag of M&Ms. "No bribes."

Tanna scowls at me but returns the candy.

"Whatever," she says, flipping her hair. "At this rate, we'll be able to retire when we're fifteen."

Our first client is a sixth-grader named Daphne Mazer. I don't know Daphne all that well, but I do know she has a dog named Olive. Everyone in the whole school knows about Olive since he's pretty much the only thing Daphne talks about. Most of her sentences start with "Olive did the cutest thing . . ." or "I really miss Olive . . ." She spends all of her free time in the computer lab, making Olive screen savers and icons. When she signs her name, she even draws a paw print underneath.

"I'm sort of surprised Daphne cares about who she's going to marry," I tell Tanna as we set up the machine. "I didn't think she cared about anything except Olive."

"Maybe she's hoping the Ewmitter will match them up together," Tanna whispers as she flips open the new green notebook she's using to schedule Ewmitter appointments.

I slide open the glass door that leads to my backyard and try not to laugh. It's hard. Especially when Daphne walks in wearing a T-shirt with Olive's face silk-screened across the front.

Tanna and I carefully avoid each other's gaze.

"That's ten dollars, please," Tanna says. Her voice is really stiff and formal, very businesslike.

"Uh, sure," Daphne says, handing Tanna the money. She points to the machine and her eyes widen. "So that's it? That's the Ewmitter? It sure is ugly."

"It's *retro*," I explain. "Haven't you ever—oh, forget it." I take a step forward. "So I thought I'd show you how it works first. You know, maybe a couple of test runs before I type in your name."

Tanna checks her watch. "We have other clients waiting," she reminds me.

"It'll only take a second," I tell her. "And this way, Daphne will know that the machine's for real."

"Fine," Tanna says, even though she's still frowning. "But let's keep things moving. No showing off."

I curl my toes into my sneakers. *Not fair*, I think. I'm not a show-off type person.

"I have to get home soon, anyway," Daphne tells us. "Olive needs his afternoon walk."

I input Daphne's dad's name, then try our principal, Mrs. Caputo. The Ewmitter easily matches up both couples.

"Wow," Daphne breathes, as the warbled strains of the "Wedding March" fill the room. I smile at her. "Ready?"

She nods. "Daphne Pauline Mazer."

The three of us watch in silence as the confetti-covered screen clears, informing us that Daphne's future spouse is someone named Lester Jerome Heckheimer.

Daphne wrinkles her nose. "Lester Jerome Heckheimer? That's an *awful* name."

At least I'm not the only one stuck with a lemon, I think, and then feel guilty. *Lester Jerome* sounds too terrible to wish on anyone.

"It's not so bad," I tell her.

"I think it sounds nice and old-fashioned," Tanna says.

"It's hideous," Daphne complains, turning to us. "I mean, really, who is this guy? I don't even know him."

"Not yet," Tanna points out. "But you will. That's the whole point."

"Maybe you should try Googling him," I offer.

"Good idea," Daphne says, but she still looks stressed. "I mean, what if Lester hates dogs?" Her face pales. "I think I need to talk to Olive about this."

"Good luck!" I tell her as she rushes off.

Tanna turns to me. "Well, that went well," she says.

"I don't know," I say, watching Daphne cut across the backyard and disappear behind the apple tree. "She seemed pretty upset. Maybe we should call her tonight, you know, to see if she's okay. I could tell her about OC. It might give her some ideas if she wants to try to change the Ewmitter results."

Tanna sighs. "Molly, we're professionals. We can't get emotionally involved with our clients." She glances at the green notebook and frowns. "Gus is next. I didn't want to schedule him, but it didn't seem fair not to."

"What are you guys doing?"

Tanna and I whip around. Milo's standing in the doorway, smiling happily.

"You can't be here," Tanna tells him. "You're supposed to be watching the driveway."

It's true. Milo's our official lookout, in case the Claw comes home unexpectedly. The job wasn't really our idea, though. Milo sort of insisted on it, right after he reminded us of his ratting powers.

"I'm bored," he complains. Behind him, I can see Gus Whitman leaning against my old swing set. It suddenly occurs to me that, other than Milo who really doesn't count, Gus is the first boy I've ever had over at my house. And even though this is the farthest thing from a date I could possibly imagine, the thought still makes my stomach jump.

"So go home," Tanna tells him. She waves to Gus, signaling him inside. "We're busy."

Tanna and Milo start to argue back and forth. I'm tempted to run upstairs, to check if Daisy Palmer emailed me/my dad back, but thinking about Daisy makes me feel guilty. I haven't told Tanna about her yet. I know she wouldn't approve of the whole "Let's email" plan. She'd just remind me how engaged people don't stay engaged and that October will be here sooner than I think. And that's something I'm really not in the mood to hear.

Besides, Tanna hasn't asked me about OC, so technically I haven't lied.

Milo stomps off as Gus approaches.

"Hey," he says to Tanna.

"Hey, yourself," she says, flipping her hair. Then she straightens. When she speaks again, it's in the same clipped, professional tone she used with Daphne. "That'll be ten dollars please. Cash only."

"Oh, uh, sure," Gus says, reaching into his pocket. He pulls out a ten-dollar bill and passes it to Tanna.

The room falls completely silent. I watch as Tanna taps her green notebook with a pen and Gus shifts his weight from foot to foot. Even though the situation has absolutely nothing to do with me, a weird shakiness creeps into my legs and arms.

"So that's it?" Gus says finally. He's staring at the Ewmitter, his eyebrows raised. "It sure is—"

"Uh, ready?" I ask, cutting him off. I don't offer to do any test runs. I want this to be over as soon as possible.

Gus shrugs. "Sure," he says.

I step toward the machine and fiddle with the dials. In a

matter of seconds, the name of Gus's future wife—Caroline Nicole Fairfax—splashes across the screen.

Beside me, I feel Tanna clench up.

"Pretty name," I tell Gus, because it's the truth and because I can't stand the quiet.

He shrugs again. "I guess."

"That's it?" Tanna asks. When she turns, her eyes are flashing and I'm surprised by how angry she looks. "You don't believe it? Do you think the machine's a fake?"

"Maybe it is, maybe it isn't," he says.

Tanna's cheeks turn red. "What do you mean?" she demands.

Gus shoves his hands into his pockets. "I don't know," he says. "I mean, it's sort of hard to get excited about some total stranger I'm supposed to like in about fifteen years."

"Then why'd you even sign up? You were one of the first," Tanna says, her voice is softer now. It's filled with curiosity, along with something else I can't really . . . wait, is that relief? Is Tanna jealous of Caroline Nicole whatever?

Gus shifts his gaze to his feet. "I just wanted to see what you guys were up to down here."

The weird accordion feeling in my stomach is back now, full force. If I open my mouth, I'll bet I'd play a song.

"Forget it," Tanna says, reaching into the cash box to pull out Gus's money. She's blinking her eyes way too much and her cheeks are flushed. "Here, take it."

Gus pauses, then slowly takes the money.

"Wow," I say, as we watch him go. "That was really—"

"Stupid," Tanna says, finishing my sentence.

I turn to her, surprised.

"I just gave away half of today's earnings," she says regretfully. "I told you we can't get emotional over clients. It's bloody bad for business." She flips open her green notebook and studies the schedule. "So, who's next?"

Chapter 14

"When someone's trying to take the ball," Julie tells me, in between bites of Sloppy Joe, "all you have to do is stop and take a quick step to the right, then go left really fast. It's the easiest fake-out, but it works every time. Just don't let down your guard. And *don't* freak out."

Tanna rolls her eyes. "Can we please talk about something other than basketball?" she complains.

"Sorry," Julie says. "We can talk about anything you want."

I stare down at my lunch but don't apologize. I know Tanna's just grumpy because I invited Julie to sit at our table.

Well, I think, biting into an apple, *what was I supposed to do?* Julie asked. I couldn't just tell her no. That would've been rude. Besides, it feels good to talk about something other than Sir Edmund and the Ewmitter. Even if it is sports.

Tanna turns to me. "I thought you hated PE."

"I do," I say. Although to be honest, basketball is sort of growing on me. It's not like I'm ready for the WNBA or anything, but thanks to Julie my skills are definitely improving. Mrs. Sixsmith hasn't yelled at me once in two weeks and last class she even shouted "Nice footwork, Paige!" during a game. When she blew her whistle at me, I knew she meant it in a good way.

Tanna pulls the green notebook out of her bag. "I thought we could go over the schedule," she says. "This afternoon's going to be busy."

I glance over her shoulder at the long list of names. "Yikes." One thing's for sure: the who-are-you-going-to-marry business is definitely booming.

"Why haven't you signed up yet?" Tanna asks Julie. "You're practically the only one left." She drops her eyes back down to the notebook, pursing her lips together as she studies the page. "We *might* be able to squeeze you in next week . . . as a favor."

"Thanks, but that's okay," Julie replies, her voice light and casual. "I don't think the Ewmitter's really my thing."

I hold my breath. I knew we'd have to talk about this sooner or later, but I was hoping it would be later, not sooner. Other than that day out on the playground, Julie's pretty much kept her Ewmitter opinions to herself. When I told her about the business, she wished me luck, but her eyes were frowning and I could tell she was worried.

"What do you mean?" Tanna asks, incredulous. "Don't you want to get married?"

Julie shrugs. "I guess so. But I don't want to know my husband until I actually meet him. In real life."

"Julie thinks the Ewmitter's like reading the last page of a book before you start," I explain.

Tanna wrinkles her nose. "I always do that. What's wrong with it?"

"Nothing, I guess," Julie says. "It's just a matter of style."

"Whatever." Tanna flips her hair and takes a long sip from the thermos of English breakfast tea she's been carrying

around with her for the past few days. "It's just as well anyway. We're totally booked."

Julie pokes me. "Molly!" she whispers, her teeth clenched. "Glenn alert!"

I turn my head as a group of fifth-graders passes our table. Glenn stops in front of Tanna and me and smiles. I'm totally stuck. There's no time for me to hide or run or even faint.

"Hi there," he says. He's wearing a red T-shirt and his khakis are a little too short, the sort of pants Tanna calls floods. When I look down his grimy sweat socks peek out at me from underneath the hem.

"Yes?" Tanna arches an eyebrow and I can tell she's annoyed. She hates when younger kids talk to us without acting intimidated.

"I was wondering if you could put me down on that list," Glenn says, eyeing the notebook. "It'd be sort of cool to know who I'm going to marry."

Panic sweeps through me. *"No!"* I shriek, and for a minute everything in the room falls silent. Totally, painfully silent.

Mrs. Irwin, the lunch lady who's supposed to patrol the cafeteria but instead spends the whole period clipping coupons, actually looks up from her Wegmans flyer. "Is there a problem over there?" she asks, squinting at us over the top of her bifocals.

Tanna, Julie, Glenn, and I all shake our heads. "No problem!" we answer in unison.

My heart whams inside my chest as Daphne Mazer rushes over. "Are you okay?" she asks me. "Do you have food poisoning?" She's been in a really good mood ever since she Googled Lester Jerome Heckheimer and discovered that his parents breed Labradoodles.

"I'm fine," I assure her. "Thanks."

Daphne moves past us and Mrs. Irwin returns to her coupons. Slowly, the cafeteria murmurs back to life.

Except over in my corner of the room. Tanna, Julie, and I are still frozen. And Glenn Borack is still standing in front of us, a perplexed look on his face.

I know I shouldn't be surprised. After all, I was sort of expecting this to happen. Everyone in school knows about the Ewmitter. It makes sense that Glenn would hear about it eventually. Still, I have no idea what to do. I *can't* let him anywhere near that machine. I nudge Tanna under the table for help.

She straightens and clears her throat. "Um, we'd love to put you down," she explains, coming to the rescue. "Only we're all booked up until summer break."

I relax. A little.

"But I thought you have a wait list or something?" Glenn pushes.

"We do, but that's booked, too," Tanna says smoothly, in her best business-is-business voice. "I'm really sorry. Maybe try again next year?"

Glenn looks so disappointed, I almost feel sorry for him. Almost.

"Wow," Julie breathes as he walks away. "That was really close."

"Thanks," I say to Tanna. "Think he bought it?"

"Definitely," she says. "He won't bother us again. Nightmare avoided."

Now I really do relax. Tanna sounds so sure of herself, it's impossible not to believe her.

The bell rings and Tanna grabs her tray. "I've gotta run," she says. "I'm doing an extra credit report on Queen Elizabeth for Social Studies."

Before I can say a word, she leans forward and kisses me. On both cheeks.

Julie and I stare at her.

"Relax. That's what everyone in Europe does," Tanna says, then rushes off.

"But we're not in Europe," Julie says after a few more shocked seconds. Even though she knows about the Sir Edmund thing, she still looks confused.

"Don't tell Tanna that," I say. "She'll freak."

We look at each other and giggle. Tanna's Britishisms usually bug me, but with Julie here I don't mind them so much.

I push my brownie toward her. "Want some?" I offer, thinking that sometimes food tastes better when you split it.

When Julie smiles and breaks off a piece, I know I'm right.

That afternoon, Sophie Kravitz is our first client.

"Hi, ladies," she says, waving her red leather bag at us as she glides across the floor.

"Hey," I say, shuffling my feet a little and wondering about the word *ladies*. It just feels so . . . wrong. At least, applied to me. Sophie's a different story. Today she's wearing skinny black jeans and a loose white top and she looks great. Definitely more "lady" than "kid." I suddenly wish I hadn't changed into sweatpants right after school. I wish I'd washed the Frizz, too.

Sophie stops in front of the machine and snorts. "*That's* it? *That* ugly thing's got everyone all hot and bothered?"

Tanna and I exchange a look and I remind myself that Sophie Kravitz is not a nice person and I really shouldn't care about anything she says or does. Even so, I can't stop the small part of my brain that's squealing, *Sophie Kravitz is in my house. Sophie Kravitz is in my house.* I'm so lame.

Tanna, on the other hand, is completely unfazed by Sophie's presence. "Ten dollars," she tells her, holding her palm out. "Cash only."

Sophie snaps open her bag and starts digging around.

A loud crashing sound bursts through the room. We whip around just as Glenn Borack races through the door. Milo trails behind him, panting loudly.

Tanna shoots him a serious death glare. "Thanks for the

warning," she says sarcastically. "You're definitely the worst lookout ever."

"He snuck past me!" Milo whines, trying to catch his breath. "I didn't even see him!"

Glenn steps in front of the Ewmitter. "Wow," he breathes, his eyes wide. "That's pretty cool."

"You can't be here," Tanna says, scowling at him. "All meetings are confidential."

Sophie narrows her eyes at Glenn and sniffs. "Um, I think I'll wait outside," she says, like she's in danger of catching some horrible fifth-grade germ.

"I'm sorry," Glenn says after she sashays out of the room. "But it's just, well, I checked around school and you *are* taking down other people's names. But not mine. I want to know why."

Great. Now I've hurt Glenn's feelings. In a weird way, that's probably a good thing since it might help with my whole getting-us-unmarried plan. But he just looks so sad, standing there in his too-short pants and yucky socks. And it's all my fault.

But what else can I do? Last night after dinner I snuck

down to the basement to check my Ewmitter reading again. Glenn and I are still matched. So are my dad and the Claw. I keep telling myself that it's too soon to panic and I just need more time, but that doesn't really help me right *now*. I mean, how am I supposed to stand next to Glenn and watch the Ewmitter pair us up like it's no big deal? There's no way.

I feel sick. Throw-up sick. Thank God Sophie left the room. Vomiting in front of Sophie Kravitz would definitely traumatize me for life.

Tanna clears her throat. "We're really sorry, Glenn," she says. "I think there's been a misunderstanding. We're accepting *some* new appointments."

I stare at her and bite my lip to keep from shouting *HAVE YOU GONE COMPLETELY CRAZY?* at the top of my lungs.

"But you see," she rushes on, "these are all special situations, which we really can't discuss, because of client privilege."

I start to breathe again.

Glenn's expression lightens. "Really?" he says. "I mean, because I thought . . ."

Tanna shakes her head firmly. "We're not at liberty to discuss our clients. Sorry."

Glenn nods acceptingly. "How about this," he suggests, his face serious. "I'll help Milo watch the driveway, free of charge. And that way, if a space opens up last minute or something, I'll be here for it."

Unbelievable. Doesn't he ever give up?

"But we're all booked," I repeat. "Even the wait list."

"You never know," Glenn says. "Besides, Milo could really use some help out there. When I showed up he was collecting rocks and talking to himself."

"It's for a school project!" Milo cries.

Tanna shakes her head and turns back to Glenn. "I seriously doubt a space will open," she presses.

"But if one does," he says, "I'll be ready."

Tanna shoots me a look that says, *Your husband, your decision.*

Never in my whole life have I met a bigger pest than Glenn Borack. Seriously. If there were some sort of Pest of the Year award, he'd win first prize. He'd even beat out the mosquito. He just doesn't understand the meaning of the word *no*.

"Fine," I snort. "Just make sure you stay outside."

Glenn smiles. "Gotcha." He heads out the door then turns. "I'll send Sophie back in, okay?"

"Whatever," Tanna says grudgingly. She watches him leave, then turns to me. "Well, one thing's for sure. You're definitely not marrying a wimp."

"Thanks," I tell her. "That changes everything."

Chapter 15

After Glenn leaves the basement, Sophie saunters back in and drops her bag on the floor.

"Ready?" Tanna asks.

"I was ready twenty minutes ago," Sophie snaps, but then, remembering she's supposed to be in "nice" mode, tacks on a "Sure, no problem," in this really sweet voice.

Tanna rolls her eyes at me, like, *Let's just get this done.*

My hand hovers over the Ewmitter's dial. "Um, what's your full name?"

"Sophia Ethel Kravitz," Sophie says, blushing the tiniest bit. "Ethel's a family name."

At first everything is business as usual. I enter the name and hit the red button. The Ewmitter starts to hum and then the weird confetti-static clouds the screen.

And that's when things get crazy.

The monitor blacks out and the Ewmitter starts to vibrate. *Really* vibrate. The machine shakes so hard, it shimmies across the floor.

"What's going on?" Tanna places her hand on top of the box then quickly draws back. "Ow! That's *hot*."

The Ewmitter jerks some more. It looks like it's trying to limbo.

"Do you think it's gonna explode?" Sophie asks. Her face is chalk-white.

"Maybe we should turn it off," Tanna suggests.

They're both looking at me, like I have all the answers. Like it's somehow my fault the stupid machine is totally spazzing out. It's actually really annoying. I mean, just because I'm the only one who can work the Ewmitter and it happens to live in my basement, I'm supposed to be some sort of marriage-machine expert? I don't think so.

"I-I'm not sure," I say.

The Ewmitter moans some more and lurches forward. We all take a giant step back.

"Maybe it's crashing?" I offer. "You know, like a computer?"

"We should leave," Sophie says in a wobbly voice. "I really think it's gonna blow up."

I try to imagine my father's face when he gets home from work only to discover that there is no more home, that it's been blasted to smithereens. All because of me.

"I can't just leave," I say, taking a small step forward. "I have to fix it."

"Be careful," Tanna warns.

Heart thumping, I reach my hand out and squeeze my eyes shut. If I can just reach the plug, maybe I can shut it down.

And then suddenly, the room's quiet again.

I open my eyes as the familiar strains of the "Wedding March" trill through the air. The flowery script is back, scrolling across the screen. Sophie, Tanna, and I stand in silence, reading the monitor:

BRIDE 💍 *Sophia Ethel Kravitz*
GROOM 🎀 *Ross Ellis Beeson*

- *Samuel Joshua Davies*
- *Geoffrey Stephen Todd*
- *Franklin Allen Hardy*
- *Eric Michael Green*
- *Grant Daniel Jameson*
- *Joseph Addison Gray*

Whoa. No wonder the Ewmitter almost blew a fuse. Sophie Kravitz is going to have seven husbands. She'll be married seven times. She's like Snow White . . . only not in a happily-ever-after sort of way. I glance over at her. Her eyebrows are tight across her forehead and her mouth is bunched into a small, round knot.

"I don't get it," she says, tearing her eyes from the screen to look at me. "Which one am I marrying?"

I shift my gaze to a spot on the wall directly above the Ewmitttter.

"I think, all of them?" I say. My voice comes out in a quiver.

Sophie's face twists into an expression I can't read. "No way," she says. "That's just not possible."

"I guess the machine thinks so," Tanna says, but not in a harsh way. She just sounds very matter-of-fact.

"Well, it's wrong." Sophie places her hands on her hips. She doesn't sound confused anymore. She sounds mad. And Southern. Normally she talks with just a hint of an accent, but her anger seems to bring it on full force. "It has to be wrong. It's been wrong before, right?"

Tanna and I don't answer.

"I am *not* getting married seven times, y'all," she insists. Now she sounds really *Dukes of Hazzard*. "That's just not happening."

I rack my brain for something nice to say. Something that will calm Sophie down and make her feel better. Not because I'm afraid of her (although I am) and not because I really want the moment to end (even though I do), but because I know what it's like to have a bad Ewmitter reading. I know how it feels to have your future splash in front of you . . . and completely gross you out.

I wonder if sharing the Ewmitter was a mistake. It's so hard to be sure. I mean, if knowing that she's gonna have seven husbands will help her *not* have seven husbands, then Sophie's reading was a good thing. Definitely.

But what if the readings are final and there's nothing anyone can do about it? What if Sophie's stuck with her seven husbands and I'm stuck with Gross Glenn and my dad's stuck with the Claw? Then worrying about all of this stuff is just a big old waste of time.

It's all so confusing. And, at this moment, not very helpful, either. The most popular girl in school is standing right in front of me, practically breathing fire, and all I have are a bunch of stupid questions floating around inside my brain. Questions, but no answers.

"We won't tell anyone," I say softly. "We swear."

Angry red splotches color Sophie's cheeks and her eyes narrow until they almost disappear.

If there was a right thing to say, that definitely wasn't it.

"You'd better not," she spits. Her face hardens. "What were the other readings like?"

I open my mouth, ready to tell her everything. I know it's horrible, but I'm in total save-yourself mode. But before I can say a word, Tanna snaps her notebook shut, startling me.

"That's confidential," she explains. "We can't say."

"I just want to know if anyone else was matched with as

many people as I was," Sophie croons. Her supersweet voice is back now. It's even scarier than the Hannah Montana twang.

"Can't do it," Tanna says firmly.

"Oh, come on," Sophie wheedles. "You don't have to tell me *everyone* . . . How about Gus? Who's he marrying?" She shoots Tanna a look. "Anyone we know?"

Tanna folds her arms across her chest. "Why don't you ask him?" she says, in this really snotty voice I've never heard before.

The two stand there, staring at each other. And I stand there, watching them.

"I'm sorry," I say finally, because I feel like someone needs to say something.

Sophie's eyes flash. "I hope so," she hisses. "Because y'all are making a big mistake. *Huge*."

I have to bite my tongue to stop myself from saying *I know*.

Sophie scoops her bag off of the floor and flounces out the door.

"What a tosser," Tanna says, flipping the notebook back open.

"A *what*?" I ask. Talking to Tanna has gotten so confusing.

"Although I guess you can't blame her for being upset," she continues. "I mean, seven husbands? *Jeez.*"

I'm having a little trouble breathing. I keep trying to picture Social Studies tomorrow. The iPhone texts will definitely be back. The whispering, too. Who knows what else I'm in for?

"The whole thing just makes me realize how lucky I am," Tanna says. "I mean, I have Sir Edmund. How great is that?"

I stare at her. I'm really not in the mood to talk about Sir Edmund.

Tanna closes her notebook and sighs in this really loud way. "Molly, you're not stressing about the Sophie thing are you?" She's talking in the I'm-such-a-patient-parent voice her mom uses with the twins. "She's just upset. It's no big deal."

"I think we're in trouble," I say. "She's really mad."

"Please. It'll be fine. Just stop thinking about it."

I try, but it's really hard to stop thinking about something you've specifically been told to stop thinking about. It might even be impossible. When Tanna leaves, I do my homework, watch TV, and answer Daisy's latest email (she loved the peach-cobbler ice cream and I send her a picture of my dad, pre-Starburst clothing). I even practice basketball—that's how desperate I am to forget. I keep hoping all that dribbling will pound the memory right out of my head.

But it doesn't work. Nothing does. My brain keeps skipping back to the whole Sophie Kravitz–and-the-seven-husbands thing.

When I wake up the next morning, my heart's pounding like I've just run a race and there's a queasy feeling slipping around inside my stomach.

And now I have Social Studies. I slide into my desk and look around. As if on cue, Sophie and Tessa stroll through the door, their arms linked. For a split second I'm distracted by how perfect they look together. Sophie's wearing a super-short jean mini *(How can her legs be so tan? It's freezing outside!)* and her bright green hoodie matches the green from Tessa's green-and-white striped shirt. Their patent-leather ballet flats are identical, except Sophie's are black and Tessa's are pink.

Did they plan their outfits or did the whole color coor-

dination thing just happen naturally? I think about what Tanna's wearing today—a fuzzy purple sweater and mauve leggings—and how my navy cords don't match. At all.

I hold my breath as they pass my desk. This is gonna be ugly. I really wish I were anywhere but here.

Only nothing happens. Nothing. They sail right past me, as if I'm invisible.

I watch as Sophie drops her books onto her desk and pulls a tube of lip gloss out of her bag. She brushes the wand over her mouth, then passes it to Tessa.

"So what happened yesterday?" Tessa says, smearing sticky pink goo across her lips.

I slide my eyes over to Sophie, but her face is buried in her bag and I can't tell what she's thinking.

"Nothing. I didn't go." Her voice is so mumbled it takes me a minute to realize what she's saying.

Tessa's eyebrows shoot up. "Why not?"

"I just decided the whole thing's sort of lame," Sophie says, moving her bag to the floor and folding her arms across her chest. "Besides, it might not even be true, so why waste the money?"

Tessa stares at her. "You're right," she says, after a minute.

"I thought the same thing when I went. Total waste of time."

I smile to myself, remembering Tessa's reading and the way she jumped all around when the Ewmitter told her she was marrying some guy named Peter Pitt. "I'll bet he's related to *Brad*!" she kept shrieking. I've never seen anyone more excited.

"Whatever," Sophie says. "I've got better things to do anyway."

Tessa nods. "Definitely."

I flip open my notebook and jot down the date, but my handwriting comes out all jerky.

Relax, I tell myself as Mr. Richards prints SEPARATION OF POWERS across the blackboard and smiles, as if we haven't been studying this for six straight weeks. *It could have been so much worse. Sophie just ignored you. That means everything's back to normal.*

But if that's true, then why do I still feel so nervous?

Chapter 16

So my chest is shrinking. Yesterday I had my second horsehair fitting and Maurice informed me that he'd have to take in the bust (I really hate that word) some more. Afterwards, I snagged a tape measure from my dad's toolbox, just to be sure. I measured last night and then again this morning and at some point between the two I lost a quarter of an inch.

That can't be normal. I almost snuck out and bought one of those what's-happening-to-my-body books, but I'm not really sure I want to know what's happening to my body. Besides, no way am I taking one of those books up to the cash register. That's way more embarrassing than a shrinking chest.

I guess it's possible I messed up with the measuring, but I don't see how. Both times I was really, really careful. I'm going to try again tonight, as a sort of tiebreaker. I just have to remember to return the tape measure before my dad notices it's gone.

"See if you can guess what I'm saying," Julie tells Tanna and me.

We're in the mall, making our way toward Candy Express, which is just about the only store I like. Tanna and I watch as Julie mouths the two words a man once shouted at my dad on the Garden State Parkway, right after they got in a fender bender.

"Hey! What was that for?" Tanna snaps. She's already in a bad mood, since it was only supposed to be the two of us at the mall. But then Julie called at the last minute, wondering what I was doing, so I invited her along, too.

It felt sort of weird, since normally Tanna and I are a pair. But I decided that lying to Julie would've felt even weirder.

"What?" Julie says, smiling innocently. "All I said was *vacuum*. See?" Her lips form the word again.

I laugh. Tanna rolls her eyes, but I can tell she's sort of impressed.

We reach the store and head straight for the bulk candy. Julie and I grab bags and start shoving them full of gummies.

Tanna surveys the selection and frowns. "I wonder if they have any wine gums?" she says thoughtfully.

"They don't sell wine here," I say, surprised. Tanna's been to Candy Express about a million times before. "And even if they did, we couldn't buy it anyway."

Tanna flips her hair. "Wine gums aren't wine," she explains. "They're wine-flavored gummies."

"Yuck," I say, dropping a few Swedish Fish into my bag.

"No, they're really great," Tanna insists. "Actually, I've never tried them before. But they're really popular in England."

I dig the little metal shovel into a pile of Sour Patch Kids and concentrate on capturing as many reds as possible. If I look at Julie now, I know I'll laugh.

"Maybe ask the sales guy?" Julie suggests.

Tanna sighs. "That's okay," she says. "I'll just get some truffles."

We pay for our candy and take the glass elevator down to the food court so we can sit by the fountain.

"How's the wedding going?" Julie asks me. Her eyes crinkle with concern.

"The elf dress is almost ready," I say, skipping the part about my deflating chest. "And last night they ordered invitations."

I wait for Tanna to say something, but she's sifting through her bag of truffles and doesn't seem to be paying attention. I still haven't told her about Daisy Palmer, but I don't feel so bad about it anymore. I can't remember the last time she even mentioned OC.

"Whoa," Julie says. "Sounds serious." She pops a handful of black licorice nibs into her mouth and chews thoughtfully.

I force myself not to make a face. I can't stand black licorice. "I'm trying not to panic," I say, "but I checked the Ewmitter this morning and the reading still hasn't changed. And there were all these travel brochures spread out on the kitchen table." I tell them about how I had to eat my cornflakes with phrases like *#1 Honeymoon Destination!* and *Get Mauiied!* floating before my eyes.

Again, I wait for Tanna to say something reassuring.

"Will you go with them?" Julie asks.

"I don't know," I say. "I never really thought about it before." It's true, too. Up until this morning, I'd never thought about the honeymoon at all.

Finally, Tanna looks up. "You should really tell them to go to London," she suggests, licking chocolate from her fingers. "It's supposed to be one of the most romantic cities in the world. I'm trying to get my parents to take us for spring break, but they say the twins are still too young."

Julie and I stare at her. Realizing what she's said, Tanna's cheeks turn light pink.

"Oh, wow. I'm really sorry, Molly," she gushes. "I didn't mean—"

"It's okay," I say, but my voice has a cold, hard edge.

"So, um, what's happening with NJ-Dates? Any news? Because if that's not working we could totally try something else . . ." She prattles on, which makes me feel even worse, since it's so obvious she's just trying to cover for having totally forgotten that my dad and the Claw are not supposed to go on *any* honeymoon.

"Don't worry about it," I tell her.

Tanna shakes her head. "No, I mean it, Molly. The Claw's history, I swear."

"Great," I say in a completely flat voice.

Tanna studies me for a minute then stands, straightening her plum-colored miniskirt. "You know," she says slowly, "I'm not so sure truffles are British after all. And all this chocolate is making me kind of thirsty. I think I'll get some tea. You guys want anything?"

Julie and I shake our heads and watch as Tanna crosses the food court toward the Coffee Bean.

"You know she didn't mean it," Julie tells me.

I shrug. "I guess so." I drop a few jelly beans into my mouth and, without really thinking, fill Julie in on the Daisy Palmer situation.

"She's like the perfect stepmom," I say, after I tell her how in Daisy's last email she confessed that her favorite kid's book was *Charlotte's Web*. "We have so much in common."

"I don't know," Julie says, twisting a lock of hair around her finger. "If she's supposed to marry your dad, shouldn't she have a lot in common with him?"

"Oh, she does," I say, though to be honest, I'd sort of for-

gotten about that part. "She's really smart and has great taste in food. I know he'll really like her. I'll bet his Ewmitter reading changes the *second* they meet."

Julie's lips dip into the tiny, barely there frown she always makes whenever I mention the Ewmitter. "So how are you gonna get the two of them together?"

"I don't know," I say, miserably. "The Claw's around *all the time*. It totally stinks."

"You'll think of something," Julie says. She reaches into her pocket and pulls out some change. "Wanna make a wish?" she asks, gesturing toward the fountain.

I shake my head as Julie tosses her pennies into the water. Shoving more gummies into my mouth, I wonder how many people actually believe that a few coins can really change anything.

When I get home, my dad and the Claw are in the living room, reading another brochure.

"Well, Mol," my dad says, waving the paper at me. "I think Anguilla's definitely the place!"

I blink.

"It's in the Caribbean," the Claw explains in a you're-much-too-young-to-understand-anything kind of voice.

"I know where it is," I snap, even though I have absolutely no idea.

"It's supposed to be just gorgeous," the Claw says, leaning into my dad like he's a down comforter.

"Am I going, too?" I ask, suddenly remembering Julie's question.

The Claw straightens. "The resort we're considering really isn't child-friendly."

"I was thinking Grandma Sylvie might come and stay with you for a little while," my father says.

I make a face. Grandma Sylvie's my dad's mother. She lives in a retirement home in Arizona that she calls "the Club." Whenever she visits New Jersey she turns the heat way up and walks around the house passing out sweaters and complaining about the weather. She also dyes her hair platinum blond and tells me I shouldn't laugh, since it'll give me wrinkles when I get older.

"How long are you going for?" I ask.

"A week," my father says.

"Ten days," the Claw says at the same time.

They look at each other.

"Mitch, it's going to take us five days just to unwind," the Claw complains.

"I'm not sure I can be away for that long," my father says. He sounds worried. "The fall's our busiest time at the office and, to be honest, I don't like the idea of leaving Molly for so long."

"Good," I tell him. "Because I'm definitely not staying with Grandma Sylvie for ten straight days."

The Claw looks at me sternly. "Molly, this is a very special occasion and you're just going to have to be mature about it."

I square my shoulders and place my hands on my hips. "I'm just being open and honest. I think that's very mature."

My father glances down at his lime-green shirt. I can tell he's trying not to smile. "Why don't we think about this a little more? We don't have to make a decision today."

"No," the Claw says grudgingly. "But I did tell the travel agent we'd get back to him before the fares change."

My father closes the brochure and places it on the coffee

table. "Well, if we have to pay a little more, we pay a little more."

The Claw pouts and I feel my mouth twist into a smile. I don't even try to stop it.

"That's fine," she whines. "But since I'm the one doing all the work I'd appreciate a little consideration. I don't want to rush around at the last minute."

Her tone is supersnotty. Sophie Kravitz could seriously learn a thing or two from the Claw.

I wait for my dad to get mad. For the first time in weeks I actually feel hopeful.

My father places his arm around her shoulder. "I'm sorry you're disappointed, Phyllis. But don't worry, we'll work everything out."

I stare at them, snuggled up on the couch together, and shove down the scream in my throat.

How could he like her after that? I wonder. *How could he want someone so awful?*

I stomp upstairs, click on the computer and log into the NJ-Dates site. I'm so mad, my fingers slam the keys. It feels good.

Dear Daisy,

Well my business trip is almost over and I'd really like to set up a date. Maybe we can go out for Chinese food? I know this great place called Hunan Park. Molly can't wait to meet you, too—but of course she won't come on our date, since that would be weird. Anyway, gotta go. See you soon, I hope.

Sincerely,
Mitchell

I squeeze my eyes shut, suck in my breath, and hit SEND. (I think. It's sort of hard to type with your eyes closed.) And then I rush down to the basement and plug in the Ewmitter. *Please be different,* I pray as I type my dad's name into the machine. *Please.*

I keep my eyes glued to the keyboard until the "Wedding March" seeps into the room. And that's when I let myself look at the screen.

GROOM ⋈ *Mitchell Simon Paige*

BRIDE *Rachel Ann Ryan*
Phyllis Eileen Kruft

I stand there for a few more seconds, staring at the monitor and fighting back another scream. As soon as the names clear, I step forward again and enter my name. Then I try Tanna's. And Gus's. And anyone who pops into my head. It's an Ewmitter free-for-all.

All of the readings are exactly the same. Nothing's changed. *Nothing*. Which means everything I've done—from writing to Daisy Palmer to being extra-mean to Glenn Borack—has been a big, fat flop. Either I'm doing something really, really wrong or it doesn't matter what I do, because I can't change a thing. None of it counts for anything. Either way I'm stuck.

It makes me want to cry.

Calm down, I tell myself. *Just be patient.*

Three minutes later I'm on my bike, pedaling toward Lions Park as fast as I can go. I only learned to ride a few years ago and hardly ever take my bike out of the garage, especially in winter. But after everything that's happened today, it just feels right.

"Forget about it," I mutter, sick of worrying about the Ewmitter. I pump furiously up the hill toward the park. My face and hands are freezing and my legs are burning, but it feels good.

I think about how nice Tanna was the rest of the day. Too nice. When we went to the Body Shop, she kept insisting that all the sample perfumes smelled much better on me than they did on her or Julie, which is just about the stupidest thing I've ever heard. And when her mom picked us up, she let me ride shotgun, which she never does.

The road curves slightly and I close my eyes as the wind whips across my face. That's probably why I don't see the huge pothole on Tremont Avenue. My front tire dips into the concrete and I can feel myself being lifted. I feel like an astronaut floating around inside one of those gravity-free rooms.

Until I land with a thud.

"Are you okay?"

I look up, dazed. Glenn Borack is staring down at me, wearing his helmet and shoulder pads. His bike stands a few feet away from mine, a safe distance from the pothole.

I can feel my cheeks flush. "Yeah, no problem," I say. I try to pull myself up then wince and stay put. My knee stings and the insides of my hands are bright red.

"I don't know," Glenn says, pointing at my bloody knee. "That looks sort of bad. Wait right here." He walks over to his bike and pulls a velcro pouch off of the handlebar. "My mom won't let me ride anywhere without a first aid kit."

I stare at him, too rattled to protest. He kneels down next to me and cleans off my knee, placing a Scooby-Doo Band-Aid over the wound.

"It's all I have," he says, apologetically. "Can you get up?"

I nod and struggle to my feet. I don't ask for help, but I know Glenn is watching, just to be sure.

"This doesn't change anything about the Ewmitter," I blurt out, before I can stop myself.

Glenn fiddles with the strap dangling from his bike helmet. "I know," he says easily.

I bite my lip. I should definitely apologize for that, but for some reason my mouth just won't form the words. And after a few seconds, it's too late.

"I guess I should stick to the swings," I tell him.

"It wasn't your fault," he says. "They really need to fix this street."

I smile at him. I can't help it. Even if he is Glenn Borack and even if he is in the fifth grade it still feels good to hear that something isn't your fault.

Even when it is.

Chapter 17

On monday morning, Rodney stops Tanna and me just as we're about to step off the bus.

"Um, can I talk to you girls a sec?" he asks.

Tanna and I exchange a look as we head back to our seats. This is strange. Rodney rarely says anything except "Mornin', sweetie" and "Have a good one." He spends most of the ride to and from school singing along to whatever CD he's playing. This morning it was Beyoncé.

"What's this about?" Tanna whispers as she drops her bag to the floor.

I shrug my shoulders and stare out the window. Ever since Saturday, things have been a little weird between us.

Rodney waits for the last few kids to file off the bus, then cuts the music and walks back to where we're sitting.

"We didn't write that," Tanna says quickly, pointing to the seat in front of us, where someone scrawled *EL is hot* across the green vinyl. "We don't even know who EL is."

"What?" Rodney asks, his eyebrows wrinkling. "Oh, that. Don't worry about it."

A few seconds pass. Tanna and I share another look as Rodney nervously clears his throat.

"So I've been hearing you kids talk for a while now," he begins, then trails off. Reaching into his pocket, he pulls out his wallet and starts over. "That's Ruby," he says, flipping to a picture in the plastic sleeve.

Tanna and I lean forward and take a look. A pretty woman with curly hair and bright gold hoop earrings smiles up at us.

"Thing is," Rodney says, "we've been dating for almost four years and I think I'm ready to take things to the next level, know what I'm saying?"

Tanna and I stare. The next level? Is he talking about a new Wii game?

"And I know Ruby loves me, too, but she has all these commitment issues." He shakes his head. "I know there's no guarantee for anything, but I was just wondering . . ."

Tanna's the first to recover. "You want to know if you should propose," she says in her most businesslike tone. "You want to know if Ruby will say yes."

Rodney looks relieved to finally be able to stop talking. "It doesn't matter if she says yes, you know, *tomorrow*. But if this isn't gonna grow—"

Tanna nods dismissively. "Three-thirty," she says after consulting her notebook. "You can come by after you drop everyone off."

I shoot her an *Are you crazy?* look, but Tanna just shrugs.

There's not much more to say. I start to offer Rodney my address, then realize he's been driving to my house every day for the past three years and probably doesn't need it.

"Please don't tell anyone about this," I say instead, adding: "And don't worry about paying us. This one's on the house."

This time Tanna shoots me the *Are you crazy?* look.

"You just gave away a perfectly good commission," she complains as we step off the bus. "Honestly, Molly. We're not UNICEF."

"It just didn't seem right to make Rodney pay," I say. I can't believe Tanna's mad at me about this. She's the one who broke the "No adults" rule in the first place.

"He doesn't even qualify for need," she mutters. "He has *income.*"

We walk the rest of the way to school without saying a word. Sometimes silence feels good—thick and smooth like hot cocoa. But this silence isn't like that. This silence makes me bite my teeth together and wish I were somewhere else.

It stays with us for the rest of the day, too. Tanna and I sit together in homeroom but barely look at each other. And at lunch, the only talking we do is through Julie.

I'm not sure if anyone else notices, but it feels strange.

Things finally slip back to normal in the afternoon, when Rodney shows up for his Ewmitter appointment. Once he learns that Ruby Lia Hill is going to become Mrs. Rodney Young (at some point), his whole face lights up. He keeps hooting and shouting things like "I just won the lottery!" and "Zales, here I come!"

Tanna and I look at each other and smile.

Thanks, Ewmitter, I think as warm tingles run up and down my spine.

I'm still smiling when Glenn ushers Max Dreyfuss into the room.

"I know the drill," he tells Tanna, fishing two crumpled five-dollar bills from his pocket.

"Do you want to see a run-through?" I ask quickly. I know I sound sort of harsh, but I can't help it. Even though Max hasn't teased me once since he found out about the Ewmitter, I still haven't forgiven him for all those armpit farts.

"Nah," he says. He turns to the machine and frowns. "That's it?"

"Yeah," I tell him, pressing my lips together. "So?"

Max shakes his head. "Nothing. I guess I just thought it'd be—I don't know. Cooler or something."

I glare at him.

"Forget it," he says. "Let's do this."

I type his full name—Maxwell Robert Dreyfuss—into the machine and wait, totally bored. Rodney's reading was really exciting, but I totally couldn't care less about Max Dreyfuss's future wife . . . so long as it isn't me.

As "Wedding March" floats through the room, my stomach growls, reminding me that I barely ate any lunch. I was too upset about the whole Tanna thing.

I need a snack, I think. *Maybe I'll run upstairs after Max leaves and grab some pretzels.*

"What's going on?" Tanna asks, interrupting my thoughts. She doesn't look confused, though. She looks worried.

I turn toward the screen. Instead of a name, the space next to **BRIDE** reads *No Match.*

The hairs on my arm stand up tall. This has never happened before. Everyone has a match—no matter how weird they are.

I chew on my lower lip and stare at the monitor.

No match.

Okay. Maybe this is no big deal. Maybe Max won't want to get married. Maybe he'll decide to stay single forever and be really happy. It's not like that's against the law or anything.

On the other hand, maybe he *will* want to get married. Maybe he'll fall in love but get his heart broken. He'll wind up lonely and miserable, living in a small, beaten-up shack surrounded by old newspapers and tons of cats.

Or it could be worse. Much, much worse. What if Max

Dreyfuss never gets old enough to get married? What if he—*Yikes.* I feel shivery all over. Because the thing is, I have no idea. I glance at Max, who's still staring at the Ewmitter. His face is as white as Elmer's Glue.

"It's just a stupid machine," I say.

Tanna pulls Max's money out of the cash box and holds it out.

"No, that's okay," he says. His voice sounds thick and froggy. "I mean, I paid for a reading, it's not your fault that—"

"Forget about it," Tanna says, cutting him off. "It's not true."

"Right," I chime in. "It was just a . . . joke. Tanna and I were bored so we made it all up. We're really sorry."

Max stares down at his feet, studying his sneakers. When he looks up, his expression is so gloomy it makes my heart hurt.

He knows I'm lying. He heard the talk. He read the screen.

It's weird seeing him like this—so sad and serious. I keep hoping he'll make armpit farts or burp-talk or laugh at me with his loud hyena cackle.

"It's okay," he says softly.

Only it's not okay. And the fact that he's being so nice about the whole thing makes it even worse. I open my mouth to apologize one more time, when Glenn Borack comes crashing into the room. Milo staggers in several seconds later.

"Code red!" Glenn shouts. "Code red!"

"What does that even mean?" Tanna yells back. "Since when do we have codes?"

Glenn waves his arms in exasperation. "There's a car in the driveway!"

Fear zings down my spine.

"We have to move the machine!" Tanna cries.

We unplug the Ewmitter and lug it over to its original corner of the basement, next to the water meter. Max, Milo, and Glenn zip out the back door as Tanna and I sit down at the craft table.

My heart won't stop pounding.

A few seconds later, the ceiling above us murmurs as the Claw shuffles through the kitchen.

"Molly!" she calls. "Can you come here, please?"

Even if she does say please there's still something really rude about her tone and I remind myself to check for a new

email from Daisy. I swore I wouldn't use the Ewmitter again until my dad's date with her was official. Only it's taking Daisy longer than usual to answer.

Maybe I did the whole date thing wrong, I think as I follow Tanna up the stairs. It's sort of hard to know, since I've never actually been on a date.

Tanna and I walk into the living room, where the Claw's stretched across the sofa. She's still dressed in her workout clothes and she's not wearing any makeup. Her brown hair is pulled back in a scrunchie and threads of gray dot her hairline.

The Claw's pretty scary all of the time, but the Claw without makeup could make Godzilla cry.

"I pulled a gluteal muscle at the gym," she announces grimly, rubbing her backside.

Ordinarily, this is the sort of thing that Tanna and I live for. I mean, what's funnier than the Claw straining a butt muscle at Booty Blast class? If this had happened yesterday, we'd laugh so hard we couldn't breathe.

But as we head out to the hall closet to hunt down a heating pad and a bottle of Icy Hot, we're not even smiling.

I can't believe I ever thought sharing the Ewmitter was a nice thing to do.

I can't believe I actually thought the readings could help people change their lives.

Well, we sure changed Max Dreyfuss's life.

We made it worse.

Chapter 18

Because the Claw's gluteal muscle is still sore and she "simply cannot deal with the kitchen," she lets me order Domino's for dinner. And even though I really don't understand what your butt has to do with cooking, I'm not about to complain. I can't remember the last time the Claw let us order in, especially a MeatZZa Feast.

Still, I barely touch my slice. I have absolutely no appetite. I can't stop thinking about Max. I really wish he'd pulled a Sophie Kravitz. It'd be so much easier to deal with the whole thing if he'd been a big jerk.

I think it's time to get out of the Ewmitter business.

"I hope my injury heals quickly," the Claw says, interrupting my thoughts. She rubs her hip. "I *have* to clean the basement this weekend."

I drop my pizza onto my plate. "Wait, what?"

"The wedding prep has now entered phase three," the Claw announces importantly as she helps herself to more salad.

My father smiles. "Well, that's good news," he says, but there's something about the way he says it that makes me think he has no idea what she's talking about, either.

I look back and forth between them. "I don't get it."

The Claw frowns slightly and lowers her fork. "Phase three is gift registry and invitation preparation," she explains, like I'm the only person in the world who doesn't know this. "I need someplace to store all the boxes when they come in."

I look down at my pizza. The little brown dough bubbles on the crust stare up at me.

"But what about all of your antiques?" I ask, struggling to stay calm.

"I rented a storage space over in Summit," the Claw says. "But there's limited space, so I have to go through the whole

collection and see what gets saved and what goes to the Salvation Army." She sighs. "It's been so long, I'm not even sure what's down there anymore."

My mouth pops open and a weird half-groan, half-snort slips out.

The Claw pats my hand reassuringly. Her hot pink nails feel like needles against my skin.

"Oh, don't worry, Molly," she says. "I promise not to touch your little activities corner."

"Uh, thanks," I say, my heart slamming against my chest.

"In the meantime," the Claw continues, "you girls will need to keep your part of the room tidy. I don't want any of the gifts or invitations getting messed up." She turns to my dad. "And speaking of tidy, your study is a disaster. Really, Mitch, do you need all those awful basketball posters? They're just so garish."

"I'll see what I can do," my father says as he grabs another napkin from the dispenser.

Normally, I'd be annoyed by this whole conversation. Not only did the Claw Mitch my dad, but she also used the word *tidy*. Twice. Not to mention the fact that she bothered him about his Nets posters.

But right now, I've got bigger problems.

What happens if the Claw finds the Ewmitter?

I'm feeling a little dizzy, then realize it's because I'm holding my breath. I don't know when I started. I exhale and order myself to calm down. Really, there's no need to panic. Chances are, the Claw won't be able to work the Ewmitter and she'll just throw it out. Maybe that's not such a bad thing either. It's not like I was ever planning to use it again.

Someone will find it. As soon as I think the words I know it's true. If the Claw tosses the Ewmitter out, someone, somewhere, will find it. And maybe they'll be able to work it . . .

An image of Max Dreyfuss skips through my brain.

It'll happen again. And it'll be all my fault. Again.

"Can I be excused?" I ask.

The Claw smirks. "I know you can, but—"

"Fine," I say, gripping the edge of my plate. "*May* I be excused?"

My dad looks down at my half-eaten slice of pizza. "That's it?" he says, surprised. "I thought you'd eat half the pie."

I shake my head. "I'm not hungry."

"Remember to put your dishes in the dishwasher,"

the Claw tells me. "Dropping them in the sink isn't good enough." She pouts. "Especially tonight. I'm really not up to a lot of housework."

I carry my plate over to the counter. I can feel my dad watching me and I wait for him to ask if anything's wrong. But when I turn around he's lifting another slice of pizza out of the box and I wonder if I imagined the whole thing. Maybe he was never really looking at all.

"I tried to call you last night. Where were you?" I ask Tanna the next morning. We're standing in front of her locker, but the hallway is so crowded I keep getting hit with overstuffed backpacks. I smoosh up against the wall for safety. "The phone rang like a million times, but nobody answered."

"My mom unplugged it," Tanna says, punching in her locker combination. "The twins found out where she hides all the candy and ate like ten pounds each. Things were a little crazy and she said the phone would just push her over the edge."

"I need to talk to you," I say, lowering my voice. "We have to get rid of the Ewmitter."

Tanna nods. "You're right," she says strongly. "I thought about Max all night. I feel so bad." She pauses as her locker door swings open. "And guilty because I'm *so* lucky."

"Right," I say quickly, because the last thing I need now is another Sir Edmund speech. "But something else just came up." I tell her about dinner and the Claw's big plans for the basement.

Tanna's eyes widen. "We can't let her throw out the Ewmitter."

"I know. We need to move it before this weekend. The Claw and my dad have book group Friday night, so I was thinking we could do it then."

"Good idea," Tanna says. She's staring inside her locker, frowning.

"I'll make some room in my closet and then we can just move it up there. It shouldn't take long." I can feel myself relax. The plan really does sound simple.

"Uh-huh," Tanna says absently as she shoves her head into the locker and starts to dig around. When she speaks again her voice is muffled. "Perfect."

"So I was thinking you could spend the night," I tell her. "It'll just be easier that way. Your mom'll let you, right?"

"Huh? Oh, sure." Tanna's digging is a little wilder now, and I can tell she's barely listening to me.

"Did you lose something?" I finally ask.

"I can't find my notebook," she says, straightening. Her cheeks are flushed and her long pin-straight hair is as tousled as pin-straight hair can get—which means it still looks a lot neater than the Frizz ever will. "You know, the green one with all the Ewmitter appointments."

"So what?" I say. "We're closed for business."

Tanna chews absently on her thumbnail. "The thing is, I sort of wrote some other stuff in there."

"What other stuff?" I ask, my voice sharpening.

Tanna sighs and shifts her eyes to her feet. "I, um, kept a log of everyone's results."

"*You what?* Wait—I don't get it," I sputter. I can feel my face pinching up, all tight and unhappy. "How could you? I mean, what if—"

"Well, obviously I didn't think the book was going to get lost," Tanna says in a voice way too snooty for someone who's just majorly screwed up. Still, there's something in her tone that makes my stomach fold over. "I just decided it was important to keep a record of all the matches."

I stare at her in disbelief. "Why?"

"I don't know. I guess it just seemed like the professional thing to do. Every business keeps files on their clients." She peers into her locker and shakes her head. "I just can't believe it's lost. I swear I had it with me in homeroom."

Our eyes meet.

"Maybe you didn't lose it," I say, even though I know she's thinking the exact same thing. "Maybe it was stolen."

The bell rings and the hallway crowds with more bodies and more noise.

But where Tanna and I are standing, we don't hear a thing.

It's definitely our worst silence yet.

Chapter 19

"**Molly, heads up!**"

This is the third time Mrs. Sixsmith has yelled at me this morning. I turn toward the direction of her voice and duck, just in time. The basketball zooms over my head and smacks the wall behind me. A hot blush floods my cheeks as my teammates glare, obviously annoyed.

I can't help it. There's no way I can concentrate on a stupid game right now. My life is just too messed up.

It took about thirty seconds for word about the Ewmitter to spread through school. There are so many different theories about why Tanna and I decided to shut it down, it's sort of hard to keep them all straight. In math class, Evan Bender asked me if it's true that the FBI confiscated the machine and put Tanna and me on their Most Wanted list. And yesterday Daphne Mazer offered to lend me Olive for a few days, in case I need a little cheering up before I go to jail. She also promised they'd write. Even Milo asked Tanna if he should hire a lawyer.

This is another one of those things that, under normal circumstances, Tanna and I would laugh about. But this week we're not doing a whole lot of laughing. At least not together, anyway. Tanna still hasn't found the green notebook and she's doing that weird, overly nice thing again. Like this morning she brought me a scone for breakfast, even though she knows I always have cornflakes. And she also made this really big deal about giving me the latest *Seventeen*. There's an article in it called "Embrace Your Inner Curl," which Tanna thought might help with the Frizz. I still haven't read it, though.

I know she feels bad about the notebook and this is her way of apologizing. But I kind of wish she'd just say she was sorry. Maybe then all the weirdness would go away.

Mrs. Sixsmith's whistle blasts through my thoughts, a re-

minder that I'm only halfway through gym class. My eyes seek out Julie, who offers an encouraging smile. At least she's not mad that I've basically forgotten every basketball tip she ever taught me.

"Are you okay?" she asks when the period finally ends. It's really hard to believe we just came from the same game. Julie's cheeks are flushed and her short black hair clings to her forehead, shiny and moist.

I'm not even a little out of breath.

"I'm fine. I guess I just didn't bring my A game, you know?" I try to make my voice sound relaxed and jokey, but I'm not sure it works.

Julie doesn't know about the green notebook yet. At the beginning of the week I kept telling myself it would turn up, so there was no need to tell her. But it's Friday now and things aren't looking so good. Still, I can't seem to bring myself to say anything. She was never pro-Ewmitter to begin with. And even though she's really not the I-told-you-so type, she did sort of tell me so.

Plus, there's another, bigger reason I haven't told Julie that has more to do with me than with her. If she knew, Julie would want to talk through the whole situation. She'd ask lots of questions, too. Like do I think the notebook was stolen . . . and who stole it. And then I'd have to deal with all of the things I've been trying really, really hard not to think about.

Still, I feel guilty hiding something this huge from her.

"So, what time should my mom pick you up?" Julie asks as we push through the doors to the locker room. She and I are going to the mall again on Saturday, which I haven't told Tanna. But since Julie's the one who invited me, I don't think it's polite for me to ask anyone else.

At least that's what I keep telling myself.

Not that Tanna has any right to be mad about it, anyway. Maybe she wouldn't even care. But there just never seems like a right time to mention it. Just like there's never a right time to tell Julie about the notebook. Or that Tanna's sleeping over at my house tonight. When did things get so complicated?

I shrug. "I don't know. How 'bout eleven?" Okay, so maybe I should've invited Tanna to the mall. But there's just no way I could have invited Julie to sleep over. Tonight isn't about fun; it's about moving the Ewmitter. It's really not fair to drag Julie into the mess.

"I was thinking we could check out the Pet Pad," Julie's saying. "My mom said I can get a kitten for Christmas."

"That's great," I tell her, but I'm not really paying attention. I'm too busy thinking about how great I'll feel on Saturday, once the Ewmitter's safely hidden inside my closet. As soon as I slide that door shut, it'll be like the whole thing never happened.

I've never been this excited to forget.

I told you I don't think it's a good *mumble*."

"And I told you I *mumble* to have my honeymoon *mumble* by a twelve-year-old."

"That's a little *mumble*, don't you think?"

"Please. Don't tell me what's *mumble, mumble.* I've been killing myself over this wedding. The least you could do is try to *mumble* . . ." The Claw's voice drops an octave and the rest of her sentence is completely lost.

I lean forward slightly, straining my ears, but from my position in the hallway just outside the den, I can't hear a thing. Not that I'm supposed to. Even though my dad and the Claw are talking *about* me, they're definitely not talking *to* me. There's a huge difference.

For the record, I didn't mean to eavesdrop. I was just standing by the front door, waiting for Tanna's mom to drop her off when my name floated into the hallway. How could I not listen? This is the first time I've ever heard my dad and the Claw argue. Sure, she nags him alot, but that doesn't really count because it takes two people to fight. Usually he just sits there and smiles. As far as I know, this is the first time he's ever pushed back.

Fighting usually makes me nervous. So nervous that my insides feel all trembly. Only this fight has the opposite effect. I keep picturing the Claw standing in the den, waving her hook nails around, while my supercalm dad sits on the sofa defending me. Even though it's night, the foyer feels sunny.

The bell rings and I walk across the hall, slapping my feet extra hard against the tile so my dad and the Claw know I'm nearby.

"Did they leave yet?" Tanna asks, as soon as I open the door.

"No. Shhh." I point my finger toward the den in warning.

"Gotcha," Tanna whispers back.

We stand there, carefully avoiding each other's eyes. I think about how badly I want all the pressure between us to magically evaporate, without having to do or say anything at all.

My dad and the Claw, wearing matching sour expressions, leave for book group, and Tanna and I head down to the basement.

"This is our last trip," she says wistfully. "It's kind of sad, isn't it?"

I unplug the Ewmitter and twist the cord around my wrist. I don't feel anything except relieved.

"Can you lift your end?" I say finally, placing my hands underneath the box.

"Okay." Tanna does the same thing on her side. "On three. One . . . two . . . wait, what's that?"

I straighten. There's definitely a tapping sound coming from the backyard. Fear zips through me as I turn my head, narrowing my eyes for a closer look. Glenn Borack's nose is pressed up against the sliding glass doors. His face looks like it's floating in the inky black night.

I stomp across the room to let him in.

"What are you doing here?" I hiss.

"Our parents have book group tonight," he says, unstrapping his bike helmet. "I thought maybe you'd let me use the Ewmitter."

"Forget it," Tanna says. "We're closed for business."

"Permanently," I add. "We were just about to hide it."

"Okay," Glenn says, like this was the answer he was expecting. "I'll help."

I shake my head. "We don't need help."

"Sure you do," Glenn insists. He grabs Tanna's side of the machine and looks at me. "You and I can carry and Tanna can direct."

"Fine," says Tanna before I have time to answer. "Let's go."

We shoot each other looks. Mine says *I could kill you* and hers says, *This really isn't a big deal.*

I swear the Ewmitter has gained weight since the last time we moved it. It takes Glenn and me almost ten minutes to lug the machine up the stairs.

"Maybe you two should switch places," Tanna suggests as we stagger into the living room. "Glenn can walk backward, since he's stronger."

I glare at her. My shoulders and arms are killing me and my back feels all sticky with sweat. Tanna, on the other hand, looks tidy and relaxed in her eggplant leggings and magenta peasant blouse.

"I'm fine," I say, lowering the Ewmitter to the floor and rubbing my neck. "I just need a break."

Glenn swipes his hand across his forehead. "I'll grab some water."

"You know," Tanna says, after he leaves. "I wouldn't mind using the machine one last time." Her eyes skip over me quickly then jump away. "I mean, I know nothing's changed with Sir Edmund, but just to be sure."

"What?" I say as my mouth drops open.

"We have time. C'mon, Molly. *You've* been using it this whole time to check your dad's reading. It's only fair."

"Forget fair," I say, placing my hands on my hips. "If you go now, Glenn will want a turn and that . . ." I trail off. The thought's so awful, I can't even finish.

Tanna grabs the Ewmitter cord. "Then I'll do it now, before he comes back."

"But he's just getting water." I step in front of the machine, blocking it. "It's not like he left for a twenty-mile bike ride."

"So what if he sees me?" Tanna says, her voice tightening. "We'll just make something up."

I shake my head. "No. No way."

Tanna flips her hair back. "I can't believe you're making such a big thing out of this, Molly," she says. "You really can be such a baby."

"Oh, shut up," I snap without thinking. The words fly out of my mouth and bounce around the room like a Super Ball. "I can't believe you invited Glenn to help us—"

"I didn't invite him," Tanna insists, her eyes wide with surprise. "He just showed up."

"It's your fault we opened this dumb business in the first place," I rush on, ignoring her. My thoughts are all jumbled, but I can't stop to straighten them. "It's like you're so obsessed with the future you don't even care about *now*. I mean, look at what we did to Max."

"Hey! I said I felt bad about that," Tanna cries, her eyes flashing.

"And you're *supposed* to be helping me get rid of the Claw," I point out. "But it's like you can't even remember."

"Oh, please," she huffs. "I only agreed to help so you'd

keep using the Ewmitter." She smirks. "Like you could ever change the reading. You *really* need to grow up, Molly."

I blink. *So that's it,* I think. *Tanna never really wanted to help me. She was just doing it for the Ewmitter.*

And then it's like a wall inside of me crumbles. All of the hot, angry feelings I've been thinking over the past few months come pouring out, rough and exploding.

"Oh, right. Like copying down everyone's Ewmitter results was so grown up!" I cry. "Do you even care if people find out about Max or, or . . ." I swallow. *"Me?"*

"Of course I care," Tanna shoots back. "I'm *here* aren't I?"

"Just because you're excited about stupid Sir Edmund doesn't make you a marriage expert or anything," I say. My breath feels all choppy and I can tell my cheeks are bright red. "And for your information, most English breakfast tea isn't even made in England. I looked it up online."

"Uh, maybe I should go." Glenn stands in the doorway balancing three cups of water. I have no idea how long he's been there.

"Maybe you should!" Tanna and I shout together.

"What's going on here?"

I whip around as the Claw enters the room, just behind Glenn.

"Why are you home so early?" I ask. My stomach tightens. "Where's Dad?"

"He's still at book group," the Claw explains. "My leg was hurting, so I decided to skip dessert and get some rest." I wait for her to say something about Glenn but she doesn't seem to notice. Instead, she shifts her gaze to the Ewmitter.

I pinch my hands into fists and stare at the carpet.

"What is *that*?" the Claw asks. "Is that one of my antiques?"

I look at Tanna, waiting for her to speak up and save the day. And then I remember her words.

You really need to grow up, Molly.

I lift my head. My heart's jackhammering inside my chest, but I ignore it and force myself to talk. "It is. We've sort of been . . . playing with it."

"I thought I told you to stay in your corner of the room," the Claw says, taking a step closer to the machine. "This old television might actually be worth something."

I close my eyes. "It's not a television," I tell her. I can feel Tanna and Glenn watching me, waiting.

"Of course it is," the Claw snaps. "What else would it be?"

An idea bubbles up inside my head. If I can make the Claw *think* the wedding's not happening, maybe it won't. It's like what Julie always says about psyching yourself up for a game. It's all in the attitude. And who really cares what Tanna thinks?

"It's a marriage machine," I hear myself say. "It tells you who you're going to marry."

The Claw puts her hands on her hips. "Is this some sort of joke?" she asks. "Because it's not very funny."

"It-it's not a joke," I say, my face growing hot. "It's right about everyone and—" I take a deep breath, "and when I put your name in, it said you're not marrying my dad."

The room falls completely silent. I watch as angry red splotches spread across the Claw's cheeks.

"Get that thing out of here," she whispers, glaring at me. "And you'd better quit while you're ahead."

She turns on her heel and stalks out of the room.

"Whoa," breathes Glenn.

Tanna turns to me. "I can't believe you told the Claw. What if she believed you? She could've taken the machine away." She shakes her head. "You're so hopeless."

A look passes between us and I know for sure that Tanna really doesn't get it. If I want her to know what I was trying to do, I'll have to explain it.

I never used to have to explain anything to Tanna.

After the Claw goes upstairs, Tanna calls her mom to pick her up early. She doesn't say a word to me either. Not bye or thanks or anything.

She leaves me all alone with Glenn Borack, too.

"Are you all right?" he asks. His face is all twisted up and he looks sort of panicked. I should probably apologize for the shouting match, but I still feel pretty shaky from the fight.

"Not really," I say, without thinking.

Glenn shifts his weight. "It'll be okay."

"I guess I could tell her I'm sorry," I say, more to myself than to Glenn.

He shrugs. "Only if you think you did something wrong."

I tilt my head to one side, considering. Glenn has a point. Yes, my stomach is in knots knowing Tanna's mad at me and, yes, I feel bad about yelling. But I definitely meant everything I said. I just wish I'd said it sooner, instead of keep-

ing it all bottled up inside until I just about exploded. That's the only thing I really feel sorry about.

So I guess I don't want to apologize after all.

I keep waiting for Glenn to ask me more about the fight, but all he says is, "I can still help you move the Ewmitter if you want."

I turn toward the machine. Between Tanna and the Claw, I totally forgot about the whole purpose of the night. And even though I don't feel like doing anything except getting into bed and burying myself with pillows and covers, I can't just leave the Ewmitter in the middle of the living room. There's no way I can move it alone, either.

I'm not sure why, but as I stand there thinking about Glenn's offer, I suddenly remember what Julie said, that day at recess: *Glenn might get cute when he's older.* I look at him. He's wearing knee pads and there's a huge ketchup stain on his T-shirt, which must be from dinner, 'cause it still looks sort of wet. Even so, it doesn't gross me out. I mean, it's not like I want to get *married* or anything *(Yuck!)* but for the first time ever, the thought of Glenn helping me—or even being around me—doesn't make me feel queasy.

He's a pretty nice guy, I guess. For a fifth-grader.

"Sure," I say, finally. "Thanks."

Glenn leans over and lifts up his side of the box. As we carry it up the stairs to my room, he walks backward just as Tanna suggested.

She was right. It is easier that way.

Chapter 20

Sophie Kravitz is having another pool party, just in time for Valentine's Day. And this year she invited the whole grade. Boys included.

Even so, I was still surprised to get the evite. Sophie hasn't spoken to me once since the whole seven-husbands incident. I didn't even think she knew my email address.

I reread the invitation like a hundred times just to be sure there wasn't some sort of mistake. But it's definitely for me. It's really cute, too, with three pairs of flip-flops on the front, all decorated with tiny hearts and a banner that reads, "You're Invited . . ."

Everyone's talking about it. In Social Studies I overheard Sophie telling Tessa she had a big surprise planned for everyone at the party, so of course Tessa immediately cried, "Oh! You have to tell me!" but Sophie shook her head.

"Nope. Then it won't be a surprise!" she said, with an *I've-got-a-secret* grin on her face. "Oh, and my mom ordered two dozen heart-shaped cupcakes from Prantl's and bought, like, a ton of candy," she went on, changing the subject. "Everything's pink and red—you know, for Valentine's Day."

Then she started talking all about the brand-new pink-and-white bikini she'd bought last weekend, just for the party. When she said the part about it being a two-piece, I noticed that she raised her voice and stared straight at Gus. He didn't say anything though, so I'm not sure he heard. But Max Dreyfuss did and made a really big joke out of it. He stuck his chest way out and strutted around the room like he was a supermodel.

"I have a new bikini, too!" he shouted. "And I'm getting my legs waxed!"

Even though it was an obnoxious thing to do, I was really relieved. Ever since that afternoon in my basement, Max has been sort of quiet.

The thought of wearing a bathing suit—even a one-piece—in front of Max and Gus makes my insides squirm, but there's no way I'm staying home. This is the first boy girl party anyone in my grade has ever had; it's really not the sort of thing you'd want to miss out on.

Still, it's hard for me to get really excited since the rest of my life is sort of a mess. Daisy Palmer hasn't emailed back and I've just about given up on OC. It was a stupid idea anyway, since there's no way this wedding isn't happening. Last night Maurice dropped off the elf dress. It's still hideous, but at least now it fits right, provided my chest doesn't do any more shrinking.

I stuck it way in the back of my closet but then moved it to the guest bedroom. Even that doesn't feel far enough away, though.

So now the Ewmitter's hidden in my closet, but I don't feel even the tiniest bit relaxed. Actually, things feel stranger than ever. Like right now. Julie and I are eating lunch together, just the two of us. And across the room, Tanna's at our old table sitting in between Sophie and Anne. Tessa's sitting on Sophie's other side and the four of them look really happy.

Tanna hasn't looked my way once.

Julie follows my gaze and sighs. At the mall on Saturday, I told her all about the fight. I was so upset, I even told her about the notebook. Julie was really great about it. She didn't ask any questions, just shook her head and told me she was sorry. She even bought me a bag of gummi worms to try and cheer me up.

It didn't work, but it was still a nice thing to do.

"Look, I don't want to get in the middle or anything," she says, chewing on a baby carrot. "But why don't you just try talking to her? I'm sure she feels bad, too."

I watch as Sophie passes Tanna her iPhone and the two crack up. It's hard to imagine that, just a few weeks ago, Tanna rolled her eyes and flipped her hair anytime Sophie was around.

They look like they've been friends for years.

I wonder what they're talking about. Probably party stuff. I'm sure Tanna's going, now that she and Sophie are . . . what? Best friends? Best friends in progress?

My chest tightens. "She sure doesn't look like it," I mutter, twisting off the top of my Oreo to scoop out the white stuff. It tastes like sawdust in my mouth.

For the rest of the day, I can't get the image of Sophie and Tanna out of my head. Because the thing is—and I've been thinking about this a lot—there's only so much I can blame on the Ewmitter and Sir Edmund. Maybe everything that's happened between us would've happened anyway. Tanna's supposed to be with Sophie, passing notes and giggling about bikinis. And I'm supposed to be with Julie, playing with kittens and eating gummi worms.

Maybe everything feels strange not because it's wrong, but because it's different. Maybe things change because they change. And that's just life.

Still, I don't have to be all smiley about it.

That night, I help my dad clean out his study. I hate to side with the Claw on, well, anything, but I have to admit she's right. The room's a total sty. The floor's completely covered with law journals and there are stacks of paper on the desk that I swear are taller than I am.

But unlike the Claw, I'm not at all horrified. It actually looks sort of cool.

"You're just like Hubert," I say.

Hubert's this little boy from a book my dad used to read

me called *Mrs. Piggle-Wiggle's Won't-Pick-Up-Toys Cure*. Because he refuses to clean up, Hubert's room is a total mess and his mother doesn't know what to do. So she asks this quirky, sort of magical lady named Mrs. Piggle-Wiggle for advice.

Mrs. Piggle-Wiggle tells Hubert's mom to stop nagging him and to let him leave his toys wherever he wants. Eventually Hubert's room gets so messy he can't even open up his door and his mom has to slide dinner underneath with a rake. That's when Hubert sort of gets the picture and cleans up his stuff.

I loved that story when I was little.

My dad hands me a Hefty bag and stares, his face totally blank. After a few seconds, he smiles and I'm surprised how relieved I am that he remembers.

"Ah," he says. "If only Hubert were here now. He could help us clean."

I look around the room. Even the couch is covered with files. "How did it get this bad?" I ask, amazed. If I didn't clean my room for a whole year, it still wouldn't be this messy.

"You know, I have no idea," he says, scratching his head. "It just sort of crept up on me."

"You take the couch," I tell him, opening my garbage bag. "I'll take the desk."

"Good idea," my dad says, giving me a thumbs-up.

We work silently for a few minutes and even though I'm cleaning I don't mind so much.

I pull open the top drawer of his desk, expecting a total disaster.

"What's this?" I ask, staring down. The drawer's completely empty, except for a framed picture of my dad and mom holding a tiny baby.

"That's you, me, and your mom," he says walking up behind me. He squints his eyes, thinking. "I guess you were about six months old there."

"But what's it doing in here? I mean, why isn't it hanging up someplace?"

My dad shrugs. "I put it there after mom died." He turns to me and skims his hand lightly over the Frizz. It's barely a touch, but it warms me up. "We can move it if you like."

I close my eyes and imagine my dad sitting at his desk, hard at work. Whenever he needs a break, all he has to do is pull open the drawer and look down at the picture.

I shake my head. "No," I tell him. "Here's perfect."

We've been working for a good hour when the Claw barges into the room.

"Look at you two busy beavers!" she crows in this super-sweet, superfake voice. "I'm impressed!"

"We're making progress," my father says, grimacing. "Molly's making sure I don't shirk."

"Well, how do you feel about taking a little break?" she asks, smoothing her hair. "There's a whole list of wedding songs I can't find on iTunes. I thought maybe you could drive out to the mall and pick up a few CDs. They're open 'til nine."

"I'm up for anything that gets me out of cleaning," my dad says, giving me a wink. "What do you say, Mol? Feel like taking a ride?"

I drop my garbage bag and rub my arms, which are stretched and sore from all the lifting. "Sounds good," I say, relieved that the Claw isn't busting up our together time. Again.

"Let's drive out to Clifton," my father says when we're in the car. "It's a little farther, but they have a big Barnes and Noble out there. Better selection."

"Sure," I say as I click on my seat belt. I lean my head

back against the cushion and turn toward the window. "Why do you guys need CDs if you're hiring a band?"

"Oh, Phyllis wants to choose a song—sort of a theme—for our wedding," my father explains. "You know, something the band can play on our first dance together. Lots of couples do it."

An image of my dad and the Claw dancing around—real slow and romantic—pops into my head. *Yuck.* I squeeze my eyes shut, trying to make it go away.

They better pick a song I hate since no matter what they choose I'll never be able to listen to it again without feeling sick. Diarrhea sick.

"Did you and mom have a song?" I ask, suddenly.

My dad smiles as he turns into the parking lot. "Your mother? Oh, no. She didn't go for that sort of thing," he says, chuckling softly. "She didn't even want a wedding—the whole time we were planning she kept pressuring me to elope."

"Really?" I ask. "I didn't know that." And then, because I don't want the discussion to end there, I add: "So why didn't you? Elope, I mean."

My father shakes his head. "Grandma Sylvie never

would've forgiven me. And Rachel's parents—you never got a chance to meet them—but they were pretty formal. I think we stuck it out for them." He eases the car into a parking space and unlocks the doors. "I'm glad we did, too. It was—" He reaches down to unfasten his seat belt. Even though he's smiling his face looks sort of sad. "Lovely. Really lovely."

Lovely, I think as I follow him into the store. *My mother was lovely.*

My father unfolds the Claw's song list. "So, let's see. I think we'd better find the easy listening section." He looks up. "Oh, great. Here's someone we can ask."

I follow his gaze and my heart freezes. There's a salesperson—a saleswoman—walking toward us. She's got curly brown hair and big blue eyes, and she looks really surprised in a happy sort of way.

Her name tag reads, HI! I'M DAISY P!

Chapter 21

OKAY, SO I can't *believe* I forgot that Daisy Palmer works at Barnes & Noble. And I can't believe she's working the late shift when my dad and I happen to stroll through the store. Of all the stupid, stupid luck.

I watch as she closes the gap between us. It's like she's moving in slow motion. Slow, incredibly painful motion.

I turn to my dad. "Um, I think I forgot something in the car," I say, thinking fast. "I'd better go out and—"

"Mitchell! What a nice surprise!" Daisy says, joining us. "I was just about to email you, and here you are!"

"Um, hello," my father says. His eyes are wide and he's kind of half smiling; I can tell he's trying to place her.

"I was in the middle of finals *forever*," she continues. "But they're all done, thank God." She turns to me. "You must be Molly. I've heard so much about you."

"Uh, hi," I say, shifting uncomfortably.

"So, did you two just drop in to say hi?" Daisy asks. Even in her Barnes & Noble sales vest she looks pretty and, despite my intense panic, a tiny flare of hope shoots through me.

It's not perfect, I think. But at least they're together. Maybe OC wasn't so stupid after all. Maybe this'll be one of those really romantic, love-at-first-sight-no-questions-asked sort of things.

"Uh, no. Well, really we—," my father says, giving his head a little shake. "I'm sorry, but have we met before?"

Or maybe not.

"I-I don't understand," Daisy says, her cheeks coloring slightly. "You *are* Mitchell Paige, aren't you? From NJ-Dates?"

My father shakes his head again. "NJ what?"

"I think I can explain." Wait, did I just say that? *Yikes.*

"Molly? What's going on here?" my father asks. He and

Daisy are staring at me now, wearing the same bewildered expression.

"I placed an ad for you," I squeak, shifting my eyes to the floor. "Well, Tanna and I did. On a, um, dating site."

"I don't understand," my dad says, his eyebrows crinkling. "When did you do this?"

"I don't know. A few weeks ago," I say. I look up at Daisy. "I'm the one who answered you back all those times. Not my dad. He's actually, well . . . um, he's engaged." I watch as Daisy's mouth drops open, then add, "I'm really, really sorry."

"So let me get this straight: you were trying to find me a date," my father says slowly, rubbing his forehead. "Even though I'm engaged."

"I was trying to find you a date *because* you're engaged," I say. My voice cracks as the truth bubbles up. "I wanted you to meet someone else, okay?"

I don't wait for an answer. I turn on my heel and run. I reach the parking lot in about thirty seconds and that's when I realize I'm stuck. I can't walk home and my dad's my only ride.

"Molly," my father says, as he pushes through the revolving door. He reaches out and grabs my sleeve. "Don't run off. Just calm down."

"I'm sorry," I sputter. "I'm so sorry. I just—I thought maybe if you met someone really great, you'd—"

"Call off the wedding," my father finishes. "And it never occurred to you to tell me how you were feeling?"

I shake my head. "You never asked," I say, as tears spill down my face. "You don't even care."

My father's arm loops around me, pulling me in so my head rests against his chest. I sniffle into his bright yellow shirt.

"I care," he says, holding me. "Of course I care."

"But you're gonna marry the—I mean, Phyllis," I say. "And everything's so . . . different."

"I know it's different," he says, stroking my hair. "But I thought it was different in a good way, no?"

I shake my head. "No."

He sighs. "I should've asked how you were doing with all of this. I guess I've been a little . . . distracted. I'm sorry." He tightens his arms around me. "I'd promise not to let it happen again, but the thing is, Mol, I'm gonna make mistakes. But you know, you can always come to me. Anytime."

I nod. "It's just hard," I say. And even though I'm not sure what, exactly, I'm talking about, my father nods.

"It is," he agrees. "I know."

We're still standing there when, a few minutes later, Daisy comes outside to check on us.

"I know it's none of my business," she says quickly. She looks at me and smiles. "But I just wanted to make sure you're okay."

I brush the last tears from my eyes and nod. "I'm really sorry. I hope I didn't mess things up too much for you."

Daisy laughs. "No need to apologize," she says. "I really enjoyed our emails, Molly."

I smile at her. "Me, too."

My father and I say good-bye and head back toward the car. He doesn't speak again until he pulls out of the lot.

"You know," he says, frowning slightly. "I'm not going to try and change your mind about Phyllis, but I will say this: no matter what happens, we're a team." He smiles. "You and me."

"I know," I say, because I do.

Chapter 22

THE NIGHT OF Sophie's party my dad drops me off at Julie's house beforehand, so we can head over together.

"Okay, you have to help me decide which suit to wear. Be honest," she says, leading me up the wide wooden staircase to her bedroom, which is covered with posters of different athletes. The only one I recognize is David Beckham, not because I'm into soccer but because Tanna's mom reads *People.*

I flop back onto the bed and—for the millionth time—wonder what Tanna's wearing to the party. I'll bet it's a bikini. A purple bikini with ruffly straps and lots of cute little bows. *Whatever.* She can have her stupid two-piece *and* her fake accent.

I shift slightly, fiddling with the top of my navy blue one-piece. It's one of my favorites, with a square neck and straps that crisscross in the back. I wore it almost every day last summer, which is probably why the bottom's covered with white loopy strings. Hopefully, nobody will look that closely.

I considered buying a new suit for the party, but just picturing the conversation with my dad ("A bathing suit? In February? It's freezing outside!") gave me a headache.

"Just pick for me, okay?"

I watch as Julie spreads three Speedo tank suits across the bed. The only thing that's different about them is the color. I'm sort of surprised Julie even cares what she wears to the party, since she hates to shop even more than I do. Still, I guess everyone wants to look good on special occasions.

"Black," I tell her, relieved that I won't be the only girl wearing a one-piece. "It'll look great with your hair."

"Thanks." Julie grabs the suit from the bed and crinkles up her forehead. "Not like it really matters. There's no way I'm going into the pool."

I nod. Julie's really nervous that one of the boys will make a comment about her chest. And I can totally relate. Not about the chest thing (last session with the tape measure revealed that mine is no longer shrinking, but it's definitely not expanding either) but about the boy situation in general.

Still, neither of us is about to miss the sixth-grade social event of the year.

"So what do you think the big Valentine's Day surprise is?" Julie asks, after she's changed into her bathing suit and slipped her jeans and T-shirt back on.

"I don't know. Sophie wouldn't even tell her friends," I say, realizing that by "Sophie's friends" I actually mean Tanna.

"I wonder why she invited the whole grade," Julie says, frowning. "I mean, last year she made such a big thing about how only *certain* girls were invited . . ."

"Maybe she was just trying to be nice."

"I guess," Julie says, doubtfully. "It just seems sort of weird, that's all."

My mind skips over the past few months, and everything that's happened. I think about the Ewmitter, Tanna and her

purple outfits, and Tanna and Sophie sitting together, all cozy and happy.

"People change," I sniff. "It's possible."

Julie's mom drops us off in front of Sophie's house, which is massive. It's ultramodern, with lots of big, square windows and shiny gray bricks.

"Your house is huge," I blurt as soon as Sophie's mom opens the door. She looks like Sophie, just more stretched out and with bigger boobs. Her pink velour sweats are supertight and look really uncomfortable, which makes no sense at all, since that's the main reason people wear sweatpants in the first place.

"Thanks, hon," Mrs. Kravitz says, flashing me a big, white smile. "We bought the place from Marvin Hamlisch."

"Wow," I say, even though I have no idea who Marvin Hamlisch is.

"Everyone's by the pool," says Mrs. Kravitz, pointing down the hallway. "I'd escort you there myself, but Sophie banished me from the party unless someone drowns." She tosses her head back and laughs this really loud horse laugh, then rushes off to answer the door. I can't help but wonder if

Sophie's mom is in the Claw's Booty Blast class. I could see them being friends.

Julie and I walk down the hall to an indoor pool shaped like a giant lima bean. The roof is all glass and the cold February sky stretches out over our heads.

"Wow," Julie breathes. "This is amazing."

I look around. The tall potted trees that frame the pool are speckled with heart-shaped ornaments and there are big bowls of pink and red M&Ms on every table. But other than that, I'm not so sure the rest of my class really knows—or cares—about the whole Valentine's Day thing. All the boys are on one side of the pool and all the girls are on the other. It's like someone ran a giant roll of invisible tape smack down the center of the room and no one wants to cross it.

Sophie, Tanna, Tessa, and Anne are standing together next to the diving board. They're all wearing the same flared miniskirt and matching hoodie, only in different colors—Tanna's is purple of course. Even though I can't see their bathing suits, I'm sure it's a two-piece parade.

Across the pool, Gus and Max grab giant fistfuls of M&Ms and shove them into their mouths.

I stare down at the water. It looks really warm and clean (which I know means that the pool is filled with chlorine and all kinds of other gross chemicals, but it still *looks* really good) and I suddenly wish—*really* wish—that the boys had just stayed home. That way, I could dive into the pool and not think about my bathing suit . . . and how it sort of gaps at the butt, where the elastic has completely disintegrated.

"So what now?" Julie asks. "We're just gonna stand here all night? Aren't there any games planned or something?"

I shrug. It does seem sort of lame, but I'm not sure diving for pennies is the sort of thing you do at a boy-girl Valentine's Day party.

Spin the Bottle. The words pop into my head so fast, I'm not even sure where they came from. And now that they're there I can't get them out. *Spin the Bottle. Spin the Bottle. Spin the Bottle.*

I sat behind a row of seventh-graders in the last all-school assembly and they were talking about that game and how you had to kiss the person the bottle pointed to. You didn't even have a choice. It could be anyone.

I glance around the room. Max is squirting soda into the water through his front teeth.

“Oh, look,” Julie says, pointing toward the shallow end of the pool. Sophie’s standing alone, an oversize beach bag hanging from her shoulder. She’s wearing this really serious expression on her face, like she’s got something important to say.

“I know I promised everyone a big surprise . . .” She trails off, her smile widening as quiet falls over the room.

“Maybe we’re gonna have relay races,” Julie whispers hopefully.

I don’t think so, but I keep my mouth shut. *If it’s Spin the Bottle, I’ll just say I have a cold and can’t play. I’ll fake a coughing fit and go call my dad.*

But when Sophie opens the bag all of my thoughts stop short. She’s holding a green notebook. *The* green notebook. My eyes search the room, looking for Tanna. Was she in on this, too?

I find her, standing between Tessa and a huge bowl of pretzels. Her expression tells me she’s just as surprised as I am.

“It’s a story,” Sophie says slowly as she opens the notebook. “I call it ‘Who Will You Marry?’ ” She smirks. “And I thought I’d read it out loud.”

No way is this happening. No way is the entire grade about

to find out about me marrying Glenn Borack. Or Max Dreyfuss marrying nobody. There's just no way.

The room is silent now. Completely and horribly silent. The Avril Lavigne CD that was playing had just ended, so the air feels extra empty. I look at Tanna, waiting for her to say something. Or do something. But she's just standing there, staring at Sophie with her mouth open, forming a little *O*.

Max Dreyfuss fakes a yawn. "Bo-oring," he says, batting his hand over his mouth. His voice sounds really jokey, but his eyes are wide and he looks sort of scared.

"Yeah," Gus says, stepping forward. "Let's do something else."

Bit by bit, the volume creeps back into the room until everyone's talking at once. Snips of conversation—"Put the music back on" and "No, read. What's the big deal?"—trickle into my ears.

Sophie smiles. "First on the list," she says, raising her voice so she can be heard over the noise. "Is—"

"No!" I cry, springing into action. I feel my feet smack the pavement and my legs pushing me forward. I lunge at the notebook and snatch it out of Sophie's hands.

"Hey!" she shouts, diving toward me. "Give that back!"

"Molly, over here!"

I turn toward the voice. Julie's waving her hands around, just like she does on the basketball court.

I close my eyes, bend my arms back and point my elbows in her direction. I release, watching as the notebook arches gracefully through the air . . . and falls short, landing a few feet in front of Julie.

I'm really, really bad at sports.

Sophie pushes past me, racing toward the notebook. Max Dreyfuss leaps over a chaise lounge and blocks her.

"Got it!"

I look up. Tanna's standing at the edge of the pool, holding the notebook high over her head.

"Give it to me!" Sophie demands. "It's my party!"

Tanna's eyes find mine. She smiles.

And then she tosses the book into the swimming pool.

Sophie gasps as a little circle of ink seeps into the water, surrounding the book.

"Oops!" Max shouts happily. "What a butterfingers. I'll get it!"

He dives into the pool without even bothering to take off his shirt or shoes.

"I'll help," Guy says, jumping in after him.

In a matter of seconds, the entire grade is bobbing around Sophie Kravitz's pool, fully clothed.

Everyone except Sophie Kravitz.

"You're so dead!" she screams, but I'm not exactly sure who she's talking to. Maybe everyone.

"Hey, Soph, watch this!" Tessa calls. She's standing at the end of the diving board, gently bouncing up and down.

"What are you doing?" Sophie yells out. "Get off of there!"

Only it's too late. Head tucked and toes pointed, Tessa's somersaulting through the air toward the water.

"Come in!" Anne shouts from the deep end. "It's so-o-o-o warm!"

Sophie looks completely outraged. And completely alone. I watch as she shoots a final, desperate glare toward the pool, then stomps out of the room.

"Aren't you coming in?" Julie asks me, dipping her toe into the water.

"In a minute," I say. Before I have a chance to think things through, I follow the stomps.

Chapter 23

I FIND SOPHIE huddled in a corner of the hallway, leaning against a huge ceramic plant holder filled with sand dollars. And even though I'm mad—really mad—there's something about her expression that catches me off-guard. It's not just the tears. Okay, maybe that's part of it. But there's more to it than that. Sitting there on the floor, she just looks so little. Like a kid.

I can't believe it. I actually feel *sorry* for Sophie Kravitz.

When she sees me, she sits up a little straighter and rubs at her eyes. "Go away," she tells me. "Leave me alone."

I think about the green notebook and a poof of anger flares up inside of me. "How could you do that?" I say. It's not very original, but it's the first thing that pops into my head.

Sophie looks up, tears streaming down her face. "You don't understand," she sobs. "I *can't* be married seven times."

"So what? You thought embarrassing everyone else would make you feel better?"

One look at Sophie's face tells me that this is exactly what she'd thought.

I shake my head. "I don't know," I say slowly. "I don't think it works that way." And then, because Sophie looks so miserable, I add, "I mean, I'm not sure how it works, but I don't think that would've helped."

"But I had to do *something*," Sophie wails, then starts to cry again. "I want to get married *once*. That's it."

I think about Glenn Borack and how I'm not so sure I even want to try it once.

"There you are," Tanna says, storming into the sky walk. She glares at Sophie. "Just because your life looks sucky doesn't mean it's okay to ruin everyone else's."

That feels a little harsh, even for Sophie Kravitz, so I say, "Um, it's okay. I think Sophie's sorry." It feels sort of weird to be talking to Tanna after everything that's happened.

"I am," Sophie says. "I swear."

Tanna glares at me. "You're actually sticking up for her? Unbelievable."

"I'm not," I tell her. "I'm just sick of thinking about getting married. We're not even in high school yet."

Tanna looks at me. She doesn't say anything but, after a few more seconds, nods.

I turn to Sophie, chewing on my lower lip. "You're not going to tell anyone about what you read, are you?"

Sophie shakes her head. "I won't. I promise." She looks up, her eyes hopping back and forth between us. "You won't tell anyone about the seven-husbands thing, right?"

"No way," I tell her.

Tanna flips her hair back. "Of course not. That's privileged information."

Sophie sighs. "Look, I'm sorry, okay? It's just—I guess I wasn't really thinking."

"There you are!" Julie shouts from the pool, when Tanna,

Sophie, and I walk back to the party. "We're playing Marco Polo. Gus is it."

"Come on," Tanna says, smiling at me. "Let's play."

I smile back. I know we should probably talk about what happened. I know there's a lot to say and, deep down, I'm still a little mad. But now just isn't a good time. It's so loud I can barely hear my own voice and, more importantly, I don't want to. I don't want to talk about feelings and friends and growing.

Right now I just want to swim.

"Definitely," I tell her.

I take a deep breath and jump.

That night, after I hang my wet bathing suit in the bathroom and get into my pajamas, I head down to the kitchen for a snack. My father's sitting at the table, eating an egg roll and watching the Nets.

"Where's the—I mean Phyllis?" I ask.

"She's at cooking class," he says, smiling. Even though we haven't *talk*-talked since Barnes & Noble, things feel better between my dad and me. Easier, or something. "I wasn't really in the mood, so she went ahead without me." He pushes the white takeout carton across the table. "Want some?"

"Sure," I say, reaching for an egg roll. This is the first time the Claw has gone anywhere without dragging my dad along, and I'm dying to know more. But when I open my mouth I hear myself ask, "How'd you meet Mom?" instead.

My father's hand pauses over the hot mustard. "Your mother? We went to college together. You know that."

I shake my head. "No. I mean *meet* meet. For the first time." I'm surprised by how serious my voice sounds.

"Oh, right," he says. "Well, I guess it was at a party. Your mom was wearing these funny wooden shoes that were sort of hard to walk in." He laughs, remembering. "She tripped and fell into a heap right at my feet."

"Did you know right away you were going to marry her?" Wow. *Where* are all these questions coming from? Every time I open my mouth, a new one flies out.

My dad's eyebrows curve. "Me? No. Not at all." He smiles and grabs some more soy sauce from the bag. "But she knew. She told me later that she knew as soon as I helped her up. She was smart that way."

I bite into the egg roll and listen to it crunch around inside my mouth. I guess not everyone needs an Ewmitter.

I head back upstairs and open my closet door. The machine's just sitting there, next to a stack of old board games.

"I can't believe you made such a mess," I say, shaking my head.

And then—okay, I'll just come right out and admit it—before I know it, I'm breaking my own rule, dragging the Ewmitter into the middle of the floor and plugging it in. After it warms up, I type my dad's name and watch as the silver bells flash across the screen, then separate.

I blink.

GROOM *Mitchell Simon Paige*
BRIDE *Rachel Ann Ryan*

My mother's name. That's it.

The Claw is nowhere to be found.

So wait, what does this mean? What happened?

Excitement curls through me as a little voice pops up inside my head, singing: *Good-bye elf dress. Good-bye heinous sword nails. Hello Hunan Park and TV during dinner.*

A picture of Glenn Borack floats in front of my eyes and my hand shoots out. Maybe my reading's changed. And Max's. Sophie's, too.

I type in *Molly* then freeze. Because the thing is, if an Ewmitter reading can change once, maybe it'll change a million times. And if that's the case—if I *can* make my future after all—then why even bother with the stupid machine?

All I need is me.

Enough, I think, staring down at the keyboard. I reach out and tug the *M*. It pops off the machine with a neat little snap. Smiling, I pluck off the rest of the keys, twist out the red dial, and rip out the on/off switch. When I'm done, the Ewmitter looks sort of naked.

Tomorrow morning I'll haul it out to the garbage.

I stare down at the pile of buttons on my carpet and smile. Maybe I'll make a necklace or something. I could use a new hobby.

I put the Ewmitter back in the closet and get into bed. Just as I'm drifting off to sleep, my dad knocks on the door.

"This came for you in the mail," he whispers, dropping a white square envelope onto the bedside table.

I switch on the light and open the card.

"My bus driver's getting married," I tell him as I read the invitation. "I'm invited to the wedding." I smile. So that's one couple the Ewmitter was right about. Good for Rodney.

My father tilts his head to one side. "That's a little strange, isn't it?"

"Maybe he just wanted to thank me," I say, then add, "you know, for being a good kid or something."

"Do you think he invited everyone he drives?"

My dad looks so confused I almost giggle. Maybe someday I'll tell him about the Ewmitter. And the Claw. And all of it. But right now, I'm too tired for explaining.

Besides, there's plenty of time.